The Nihilist:

A Philosophical Novel

John Marmysz

NFB
Buffalo, New York

Copyright © 2015 John Marmysz
Printed in the United States of America

Marmysz, John

The Nihilist/ Marmysz- 1st Edition

ISBN: 978-0692490990

1. The Nihilist 2. Nihilism 3. Philosophy
4. Punk Rock 5. Marmysz
7. No Frills.

NFB

<<<>>>

No Frills Buffalo/Amelia Press
119 Dorchester Road
Buffalo, New York 14213

For more information visit
nofrillsbuffalo.com

I dedicate this novel to Juneko Robinson. Her love is the most stable and lasting thing that I have discovered in an otherwise impermanent world.

Contents

CHAPTER ONE: MOTHER

I.

My mother died when I was well into my 40's. Already an adult, with adult responsibilities, I was nevertheless unprepared to deal with this event.

As a philosophy professor who regularly teaches about the deaths of Socrates, Heraclitus, The Buddha, and Jesus, I'm accustomed to thinking about mortality. Despite all of this intellectual preparation, however, the death of my mother arrived as something shocking and unfamiliar. No amount of thinking or preparation, it seems, could have made it any less terrible.

People who saw her body said that she looked peaceful after she was gone, but that was because they hadn't witnessed the physical suffering that preceded her passing. Dementia had set in, taking from my mother her short-term memory but leaving her with recollections from long ago. She spoke vividly of her father, the days when she met my father, of her long dead pet dog and of my childhood, but she was unable to remember where she lived, what I did for a living, why I had to leave her house during the day and how long I would be gone before returning.

Her body deteriorated along with her memory. Her hands and knees became gnarled with arthritis. She lost feeling in her legs and she could not walk unassisted. As she became more and more debilitated, she needed help bathing and going to the bathroom.

Eventually, she barely left bed and stopped speaking. Words failed, and the only communication that passed between us was conveyed through our eyes, or when my mother would reach out with her hands and cradle my face in her palms.

The last day of her life, I took the advice of a friend and sat by my mother's bed, telling her how much I loved her, regardless of the fact that she, at this point, did not register any visible signs of recognition. Later that day, when I came back from work, the rhythm of my mother's breathing had changed, becoming more labored. Soon afterward, she stopped breathing altogether.

II.

I think about my mother every day. I think about particular episodes from the past, about both the wonderful and the hurtful words that were spoken between us, and about the dreadfulness of her suffering. Regardless of the fact that she no longer is here physically, however, she remains present in other ways. In spite of her absence, her presence still dwells with me.

I've been told that you have to move on after the death of a loved one; that you have to think of other things. But the truth is that the world I inhabit will always be infused with my mother's presence. There are, of course, the concrete memories of her face, her way of speaking, her way of laughing. More important, however, is the reality of how my actual consciousness as a whole has been shaped, formed and, ultimately, given existence by my mother.

Not only did my mother give me physical being, she shaped and nurtured my mental being. There is in me a trace of her. This trace is like a thread that, as it emanated from her world, weaved its way into my own world. Now that her end of the thread has been cut, like the umbilical chord that was cut at the moment of my birth, I am forced to go forward in life, terrified and free from the tether that previously provided me with some sense of security.

My mother created me, and over the course of the years that I have been alive, her world has been a part of my world. Even when distant from one another, she was there with me in ways that I did not realize at the time. Death, in some ways, feels like an amplified form of the separating distances we all experience when apart from one another in life; but there is a difference.

When my mother was alive, I always felt that there was a place to which I could return, a place where there was someone who cared and to whom I was responsible. I felt as though there was someone who I might disappoint and who would judge me, but who nevertheless would always be there. That feeling has now disappeared. With the death of my mother that security has been taken away, just as Nietzsche tells us that God has been taken away from the modern Western world.

I don't anticipate ever being done with my mourning. It remains an ongoing event that, to some extent, occurs everyday.

III.

The struggle to become reconciled with death is vain, both because the experience of past deaths must remain a part of one's consciousness, and because we are doomed to re-experience the deaths of others, again and again until the point at which we ourselves also die.

IV.

When I was younger, my mother and I would take walks in the woods, sharing our thoughts and discussing ideas. There was one lake in particular that we enjoyed circling. The trail around one side of the shore was open to the sky while the trail around the other side was sheltered by trees. Once we traveled the circumference of this body of water, I would experience a feeling of completeness and accomplishment. This feeling was fostered by the contrast between the shelter of the forest canopy and the expanse of sky beyond the forest. At the completion of our walks it was as if we had come full circle; the end of the trail wound back to its beginning in an unbroken circuit. As we began the walk, the woods sheltered us from the sun or the drizzle (depending on the weather conditions) until releasing us back into the openness of the sky past the tree line. We knew our walk was over once the shadows of the forest had receded and the blue color of the sky, or the grey color of the clouds, reappeared to welcome us back to the world beyond our conversation. The variation of heavens against earth, dark against light, spoken word against silence, were all signs of a predictable and comforting regularity in this routine. It was a routine that allowed us, at least for the duration of the walk, to remain distracted from the rest of the world.

V.

"I don't care what you decide to do in life," my mother said to me on one of our walks. "You can be a bum, a derelict or a hobo if you so choose. All I ask is that you be an *educated* bum.

"So it wouldn't bother you if I decided never to have a regular job for the rest of my life? You wouldn't be ashamed of me if I decided to ride the rails, or live in the woods instead of making money and buying a house?"

My mother chuckled. "I would never be ashamed of you for doing what you really want to do. The only thing is, I want you to know what it is that you want and why you want it. Don't be like so many people from my generation who never questioned their lives. There's so much stupidity in the world that stems from just that sort of mindlessness. There are so many people who just plod through life with no sense of where they are going or why they are headed in the direction they are traveling. Educate yourself. Discover what you think is important and pursue it. If you do that, even if you are penniless at least you'll have meaning."

"What if I question myself and find that I can't discover any answers to my questions?"

"Then," my mother smiled, "you'll be like Socrates! What mother wouldn't be proud to have Socrates for a son?"

VI.

We stopped along the trail to take in the lake view. Sun glinted off of the water, making it appear as if there were white speckles atop the blue waves. From our vantage point we could see the other shore and the dusty, dry, tan colored hill that acted as a sort of backdrop to the waters. Ducks swam away from us, heading toward the hill. The waves made a lap, lap, lapping sound. I could see insects flying through the air, just over the surface of the lake, in small clouds and individually. Periodically, creatures would pop up from beneath the waters momentarily, disappearing just as quickly as they appeared. I imagined that they were fish or turtles hunting for insects.

The two of us, my mother and I, were part of this scene as well. I imagined the ducks and the insects and the fish and the turtles looking back at us and wondering what we were up to.

"This is where I want you to spread my ashes when I die," my mother said. There was no hint of sadness or melancholy in her voice as she spoke these words; just a matter of fact report of her wishes. "It's very peaceful here."

VII.

When I was a child, my mother treated me with a mixture of stern discipline and indulgent attention. I always retained the sense that my mother was in charge, but I also always knew that she did not want to shield me from either the ugly or the beautiful realities of life.

"I don't want you to be sheltered. There's a lot in the world to explore. However, you have to be careful. Don't let yourself become brainwashed by what others tell you it is you should be doing. You should be aware of what is out there, but don't let it control you. You must always control it."

In line with this philosophy, my mother allowed me to view films, read books and experience art that most parents would probably consider inappropriate for children.

I recall venturing into a bookstore one afternoon and seeing a magazine behind the cashier's counter titled *Violent World*. I had read a review of this magazine in the newspaper the previous Sunday. The review denounced the magazine as "sick" and "degenerate." Apparently the entirety of *Violent World* was dedicated to photographs and stories dealing with death, dismemberment and destruction. The cover of this particular issue boasted the headline "101 Plane Crash Victims!" These words were printed over a black and white photograph of a dead body that appeared to be hanging from a tree by the torn flesh of its torso. It had no legs; the body ended just below its abdomen. The skin of its stomach spread out like a ripped blanket, catching in the branches of the tree, leaving the head and arms suspended upside down as though reaching out for the ground. I was fascinated by the lurid nature of the cover and further intrigued by the fact that the local paper had denounced this publication for its "degenerate" content. This was not the sort of reading material that good middle-class parents would allow their children to peruse.

I asked, "Mom. Can I buy that magazine?"

Without a word of approval or of disdain, my mother paid the cashier and handed me issue number three of *Violent World*.

I poured over that magazine, reading every single bit of text. I learned about the worst plane crash in history and stared for hours at the explicit photos documenting the tragedy. I read about a boy whose head was speared on a fence post when he fell from the roof of his family home, and I stared for hours at the photo accompanying the article.

I also became fascinated by a short news brief that had no

photo accompanying the story. The brief gave an account of a new fashion fad in Britain. Apparently, British kids had taken to piercing their cheeks with safety pins and dressing in torn clothing. They dyed their hair outrageous colors, and instead of dancing to music on Saturday nights they would go to nightclubs where they would jump around and smash into one another until they fell to the ground bloody and unconscious.

"I don't believe it," I recall thinking. "Why would anyone do that?"

When we had visiting relatives from Scotland stay with us that summer I asked them about this new fad.

"Aye," my Aunt confirmed, "It's true. The kids do some awfully queer things. Punk Rock, they call it. Can't say I understand it."

VIII.

My mother and I traveled to the UK a number of times over the years, mostly to visit relatives but also, I came to realize, so that my mother could strive to recall her past. The irony was that as she became older, and as her innate capacities for memory failed her, the country where she was born and where she grew up kept changing so that it was beyond easy recognition. It was as if Scotland was playing a hide-and-seek game with her, presenting hints of the past in her old neighborhood, the movie theatre where she went on her first date with my father, and the dance hall where she spent her Saturday nights as a teenager, but also concealing these things behind a veil of deterioration. The old neighborhood stood in its same location, and yet it now had razor wire fences and spray painted walls that never would have been tolerated when she was a child. The movie theatre where my father took my mother on their first date still remained, but instead of foreign films it now showed pornography. The dance hall where my mom would dance with her friends now catered to punk rockers.

It was all there, but different. Decayed.

Our last visit, a couple of years before my mother's death, was for me an unexpectedly profound experience. We visited all of the usual sites, my mother recounting how things used to be and expressing sadness for what they had become. But this time around I found myself moved by a deep sense of how this place, with all of its decay and all of its past glory, represented my own origins. Just as I would never have existed without my mother, my mother would never have existed without this place. I was rooted, through her, in this world.

IX.

Though its superficialities are in constant, unending change and flux, the world itself, that event that encompasses all of the details of reality, is always there, ever unfolding and ever present. I'm not sure what measure of comfort this can possibly offer, but I can see that the process of dark passing into light, night passing into day, sound passing into silence and present passing into past are all signs and symptoms of an ongoing movement that transcends, and yet also seems to depend upon, the details of everyday life. To grasp this idea in my understanding is to grasp a thought that feels profound, though it is not necessarily consoling.

The idea that the world consists of an ever unfolding succession of details leads my mind backward to contemplate past history, encouraging me to trace out the contours of events that have culminated in my "now." That each superficial moment of my life is a crescendo articulating and consolidating all that has ever transpired roots me to a past that I have never consciously experienced, but which nonetheless helps me to understand how I became what I have become. A sense of resignation accompanies the feeling of awe that this thought inspires in me. I feel full at the same time that I feel helpless; momentous at the same time that I feel fatalistic.

I am all that I have become.

X.

I spread my mother's ashes on the shore of the lake as she wished. However, it seemed appropriate that I save some of her remains so that they could be returned to the land of her birth.

The next year my wife Colleen and I traveled to Scotland, bringing with us a small portion of my mother's ashes to be spread at the top of a grassy hill outside of Glasgow. This had been the spot where my mother, many years before, had spread her own father's ashes after his passing.

As we stood there, not really knowing what to say, I started to cry. A year after her death, and here I was still crying. The feeling was infectious, and Colleen also began to cry, so we stood there, weeping together until our tears came to an end.

And it was then, as my tears stopped, that I first experienced this awful pain in my gut. It was a burning sensation that seemed to emanate from my stomach and to creep up through my chest into my throat. Very quickly, the pain became intense, provoking a feeling of nausea.

"I think I'm going to be sick," I said to Colleen, and I kneeled on the ground, preparing to vomit.

But nothing happened. The wave of nausea passed, the burning feeling in my chest and gut subsided, and I was back to feeling normal in a matter of minutes.

"Are you OK?" Colleen asked, her hand on my shoulder, her voice thick with concern.

"I think so," I responded. "I think I'm fine. I think it has passed."

CHAPTER TWO: THE PHILOSOPHY PROFESSOR

I.

As I was cut loose from the past, I became hopelessly re-entangled with it.

II.

There was a shameful and embarrassing secret that I kept all through the time I cared for, and then mourned, my mother: it was that I looked forward to the end of the whole ordeal. I cherished the thought of finally being free to move forward, irresponsibly, and to cease feeling dutiful. I anticipated being able to do and say the things that I never before dared when my mother was alive. I would run away. I would drink. I would take drugs. I would fuck. I would steal. I would destroy. I would subvert all moral systems. I would become the Antichrist. Once this was all over, I would do anything I wanted; and then be truly happy!

Quite silly, these thoughts; but, from what I understand, not unusual. They were the fantasies of someone overwhelmed by confused feelings of responsibility for, and devotion to, someone he loved. It was a reaction formation. I felt crushed by responsibility, debilitated by despair, and so I desired the exact opposite of these things. I engaged in the fantasy that without my mother's external presence, I would be liberated from her influence altogether. Of course this was not true. Her internal trace remained woven into my core.

Instead of running wild in the wake of my mother's passing, I found myself participating in the very same routines that had always served so well to distract me from my forlornness and to channel my deepest fears and impulses constructively. I became ever more devoted to my career as a philosophy professor, never quite recognizing that philosophy functioned as my therapy. It always had, but after my mother's death, its therapeutic nature became at once both more pronounced and more obscure.

III.

Many of my own teachers approached the subject of philosophy as an academic subject like any other, and so they recited facts, presented their own arguments and pontificated in class, all the while expecting us accurately and carefully to record the detailed information conveyed in their lectures. Such teachers treated philosophy as if it consisted of a particular body of information to be mastered.

I never viewed philosophy in this way. Even as a student, I knew that there was something more important here; something that went beyond words and that became manifest most authentically when lived, experienced and integrated into one's being.

To me philosophy never was a particular body of information but more like an open-ended process of ongoing questioning, speculation and interpretation. Strictly speaking, I do not think that there is any specific content or information that is necessary to the field of philosophy. The true philosopher is an individual who strives to take nothing for granted and thus is willing to question and explore anything at all. No specialized knowledge is required in order to engage in philosophy. Anyone can philosophize, so long as he or she is willing to think things through carefully, reasonably and deeply, all the while remaining friendly to the potential for never-ending questioning.

It is the openness of philosophical inquiry that comforts me and that serves a therapeutic purpose during my darkest moments. This may seem odd, since as I've described it, philosophy really does nothing except to provoke questioning and uncertainty. And yet, this is precisely what helps me. Philosophy encourages me to take nothing for granted, and in doing so I find myself moving toward an odd form of deliverance. When I am forlorn, philosophy gets me to question why it is so, helping me to wonder what my despair reveals, and how it is that I can become a conduit for this Truth. As this Truth courses through me, I begin to sense how insignificant I am. This is a kind of therapy that helps to combat the sort of arrogance, which becomes especially pronounced in times of despair, telling me that I am entitled to comforting answers. On one level this is unsettling; the farthest thing from therapy that one can imagine. On another, it is the best sort of therapy, since it has slowly changed my being into something more yielding to the universe and its rhythms of birth and decay. All things come and go, including my own moods and feelings, my own attachments, loves and hopes. I am nothing but a clearing in the fabric of the universe where all of these dramas transpire; and I have relinquished the conviction that I am destined to master the world's mysteries.

Socrates, my mother's hero, claimed that the highest wisdom consists in being able to recognize your own ignorance. I still believe that Socrates is perhaps the greatest of all philosophers.

IV.

The word "philosophy" means "love of wisdom," and while they do aspire toward the Truth, philosophers also always recognize how far removed they are from the ultimate and absolute truths about reality. In order to love something, there must be a separation between the lover and the object that is loved; and so it is with the lover of wisdom. A real philosopher is not an individual who knows the Truth, or an individual who possesses wisdom, but is rather a person separated from the Truth and who is thus endlessly aspiring toward wisdom. This recalls, once again, Socrates, that ugly, self-described "gadfly" who confessed that the only truth he knew for certain was that he knew nothing.

If cast in this manner, the discipline of philosophy must be understood as a never-ending process in which a person ceaselessly aspires toward, but always fails to possess, the Truth. It is a way of thinking that tolerates the deferral of final answers and is enthusiastic about ongoing questioning. For the authentic philosopher, the desire for Truth is inexhaustible, and yet the Truth is forever out of grasp.

This is nihilism; and while I learned from my mother to embrace this view, more than a few of the students that I work with find it frustrating and terrible.

Many students wonder, if the Truth that philosophers are after is impossible to possess, then what is the point of pursuing it? If philosophy really is an endless process that consists of ongoing questioning, then why philosophize? Why strive after something that you can never have? Why not just rest satisfied with what we now think?

As a professor, I respond to these sorts of questions by pointing out the instrumental importance of questioning our pregiven assumptions about the world. For one thing, without the willingness to raise new questions, there are no new answers, and without the drive to find new answers, human knowledge would stagnate. Philosophy, by encouraging us to question old truths, opens up space for new discoveries, and thus it drives human understanding forward.

In fact, the very idea of progress may be tied to the vain drive for absolute Truth. To have progress, we must have a goal toward which we are moving. Even if we never reach our goal, there is still value to be discovered in moving closer to our target. In its vain admiration for the Truth, philosophy gives us something to shoot for. Furthermore, in placing this final goal infinitely far away, philosophy makes infinite progress possible as we endlessly strive to reach something beyond our grasp.

The most important reason that I believe philosophy is productive, however, is because of its relation to humankind's most fundamental nature. We all are mortal, time-bound organisms who fear death. Philosophy, in aspiring toward the absolute, gives us a way to confront our finitude. Though we are all doomed to die, with philosophy we are granted the opportunity to think ideas that are larger than ourselves. When we philosophize we find ourselves oriented toward thoughts and ideas of the infinite and the eternal. To linger, if just for a short period of time, in the presence of these ideas is invigorating and gives us confidence that even though our bodies must die, there are principles that will exist forever.

Philosophy reminds us who we are. We are animals that endlessly aspire to overcome ourselves. We are creatures torn between the desire for stability and dissatisfaction with what we have. Being human is, in its very core, a conundrum, and it is the process of philosophizing that best gives expression to this condition.

V.

One of the philosophers we discuss in class each semester is Heraclitus. Heraclitus was an ancient Greek, Presocratic philosopher who lived some time around 500 BC. His ideas offer an ancient expression of one of the most dramatic and recurrent themes in the history of philosophy; namely that the world as we experience it always hides and covers over its deepest Truth. The more that we attempt to possess and solidify this Truth, the more it slips through our fingers.

For Heraclitus, fire offers the perfect metaphor to encapsulate this insight.

Fire is an element that, on the one hand, has a distinctive form and physicality about it. It reaches upward and moves, spreading from location to location. We can see a flame as it blazes and flutters. If another object comes into contact with a flame, it will be burned. Fire, it seems, really does have a tangible existence in the world, occupying space and producing effects on the things surrounding it.

However, fire is also rather ghostly and mysterious. It seems to come into existence out of nothing and when extinguished it disappears into nothing. If you try to grab hold of fire, your hand passes right through it. In these ways, a flame seems almost unreal and intangible.

Fire, then, is an enigma. It is powerful and potent at the same time that it is yielding and delicate. It both exists as a physical, tangible entity and as something less than physical and tangible. Today, scientists tell us that fire is a *process* of oxidation and that this process manifests itself in the visible phenomenon we call a flame. This modern way of speaking gets very close to the point that Heraclitus seems to have been driving at.

VI.

The world is fire, according to Heraclitus; not literally, but metaphorically. The various phenomena that we see, taste, touch and feel are in eternal flux. They result from an underlying tension that describes the fundamental, and yet invisible, foundation of reality.

The visible, tangible world erupts out of a conflict between hidden, opposing forces. Just as fire springs forth from and consumes substances that are cooler than it is, so too do all of the phenomena of reality spring forth from contradictory and conflicting elements. Our world exists because of the opposition between night and day, male and female, dark and light, wet and dry, etc. Without these points of conflict, the world as we know it would cease to exist, like a flame that has no fuel from which to draw. When we observe the objects that surround us, we see for ourselves that nothing remains stable once and for all. Like a flame that sparks into existence, burns and then puffs into nothingness, the universe is an unfolding process that depends on conflict, incongruity and discord for its fuel.

VII.

Heraclitus was referred to as the "dark one," partly because of his obscure and metaphorical writing style, but also because of the potentially depressing implications of his world-view. If it is true that the universe is in eternal flux, like a burning flame, then nothing is ultimately stable or lasting. All things must pass away.

"We cannot step into the same river twice," Heraclitus wrote.

Not only is the universe like a burning fire, then, it is also like a flowing river whose waters are always in motion, never resting. Everything we love and hate; everything that we enjoy and that we merely endure; all of these things are temporary. Nothing is permanent. Our lives are lived in a state of impermanence.

Both fire and water, seemingly contradictory elements, offer appropriate metaphors for reality because they call to mind the transitory nature of existence. This is the sad truth about our world according to Heraclitus. Everyone and everything in the universe will expire.

VIII.

Heraclitus' personality was obnoxious and his opinion of his fellow human beings quite low. He is reputed to have stated that he would like to see everyone in his community hanged; everyone except the young, who should inherit society and build it anew. He believed that most people are stupid and vain, living life in the pursuit of base desires. For this reason, Timon referred to Heraclitus as "the reviler of the mob."

Heraclitus died after having himself buried underneath a pile of cow manure. This seems to have been intended as treatment for some sort of disease, but it also is the perfect end for a philosopher who thought the world was shit.

IX.

In one class, during our conversation about Heraclitus, an especially attentive student remarked, "But if everything comes from the conflict of opposites, then I don't think it is true that *everything* is temporary and in flux. Really, underneath it all there is something that is stable; namely fundamental conflict."

"Excellent thought," I responded. "Heraclitus himself does at points suggest something of this nature. He vacillates between the claim that nothing is constant and the claim that conflict itself is constant."

The student turned this over in his head momentarily and then said, "So I guess you could say that the only thing that is constant is that nothing is constant."

"Spoken like a true Heraclitean!"

A wave of laughter swept over the class. As a whole, it seemed that this idea resonated with them.

"Heraclitus claims that even though the universe emerges from conflict, and even though the particular events and occurrences that take place in the history of the universe are transitory, in the aggregate, the universe just is the sum total of these occurrences. The universe, ultimately, is one thing. It is the flux and the transition and the conflict that we see around us."

The students were quiet, but it was palpable that they wanted to hear more. Their faces stared back at me in rapt attention. There were no side conversations, and everyone in the classroom seemed mentally focused on the same point of interest.

"Imagine that you could step outside of the universe in order to see it once and for all. Of course you can't really do this, but just imagine for the moment that you can. If Heraclitus is correct, what we would see is something like an intricate web of interrelated tensions that result in a single, overarching phenomenon that is the universe. Just as a painting emerges out of the various colors, textures and materials that are juxtaposed with one another on a canvas, so too the universe emerges out of the various conflicts, incongruities and strains that are manifest within its confines. When you focus on the details of a painting, you run the risk of failing to understand how all of those details harmonize with one another in order to produce a piece of art. Likewise, if you focus solely on the particular and unique events in the history of the world, you run the risk of failing to see how all of those events contribute to the unity of existence."

One student, suddenly very excited, raised her hand and simultaneously spoke up.

"That's like music! A piece of music is made up of the harmonies and rhythms that emerge from the contrast between various musical notes. You can't appreciate a musical score unless you're able to trace the connections between the notes. The experience of music requires that you step outside of any particular moment in order to experience the whole. But the whole just is the parts and their connection to one another. Is Heraclitus saying that the universe is like a musical performance?"

I felt myself swept up in the enthusiasm of this student's insight.

"Yes! Heraclitus, in fact, at one point uses the metaphor of a lyre to characterize the nature of reality. The world is like a fire, it is like a river, but it is also like a lyre, which is a stringed instrument, sort of like a harp. The only way that the lyre can produce music is through the tension of its strings. If the strings went slack and there was no tension, there would be no music!"

"I like that!," the student exclaimed. "The world is like a song! But when you put it that way, I don't see what's so dark and depressing about Heraclitus. In fact, I think his idea is quite beautiful."

I thought for a moment. The student was right. Characterizing the world in this manner seemed less sad and more wondrous than I had previously suggested.

But then I remembered the underlying issue.

"Yes," I responded, "but every piece of music must come to an end."

Saying this I smiled, and felt a twinge of heartburn in my chest.

X.

Fire is vital. Fire is powerful. Fire is useful. Fire cooks our food, it heats our homes and it runs our vehicles. It entertains us when harnessed in fireworks.

But fire is also fragile and temporary and destructive. Fire disfigures people, ignites bombs and burns down cities.

Fire has a multitude of capacities. It is neither good nor evil. It means nothing. It burns blindly, reaching upward until the fuel from which it draws has been exhausted. When extinguished, it leaves behind ashes and charred remnants as the only evidence of its past existence.

Life is like fire.

Chapter Three: Passion

I.

We were teenage punk rock lovers on fire with passion; entwined as we explored each other's physical topography with our hands and mouths. We were sweating and groaning, sliding over one another as we smiled and laughed, grimaced and moaned. Time and space were illusions during these moments when Colleen and I melted into one another.

II.

"I hope you and Colleen are behaving yourselves," my mother said to me one evening after I had come home from a date.

"What do you mean?" I asked, all the while knowing very well what she was getting at. She was afraid that Colleen and I were sexually involved. The fact of the matter was that on that very evening we had been sleeping together; multiple times in fact, one time after another. Typical horny teenagers, we had spent hours tangled within each other's embrace, climaxing, recovering, and starting it all over again. Our bodies were raw and irritated from being rubbed together and yet despite this, we craved more. We wanted to fuck one another again, and again, and again, and again...

"You know what I mean. I hope you two are being moral. I

don't want to have grandchildren just yet!" my mother warned, sternly glaring at me.

My mom saw right through me and knew exactly what was going on. I tried to keep some distance between the two of us, as I was sure that if we got any closer she would be able to smell the scent of sex on me.

"Mom!" I nervously exclaimed. "Nothing is going on! We're friends!" I pleaded, feeling embarrassed, ashamed, indignant and angry all at once.

III.

Colleen and I met when she was 16 and I was 17. Both of us had graduated early from high school and were enrolled as students in a social deviance and problems class at the local community college; a fitting place to begin our particular romance.

We would spend hours drinking coffee and talking at a cafe not far from the college. Oftentimes we would skip class just so we could sit a bit longer, say a few more words and relate just few more ideas to one another. It was a time in our relationship when the most important thing was just to be around one another. It was a time when curiosity and interest drove us to be patient, to linger together and listen to each other.

If we weren't sitting in class or at the cafe, we were riding around on my motorcycle or driving around in my big American car; an Oldsmobile Cutlass Supreme. As with our conversations, our motorcycle and car rides had no necessary destination or duration. They went on as for as long, or as shortly, as seemed appropriate to our moods or desires.

IV.

"What is the most important thing in the world to you?"

Colleen asked me.

"My integrity," I responded. "I never want to become a drone, one of 'them'. What about you? What is the most important thing in the world to you?"

"I want to make the world a better place."

V.

Walking down the street on this particular evening everything felt fine. I wasn't thinking about how much I hated the people in the world or how unhappy I was with life. Instead, I was with Colleen; beautiful, young and intelligent. She was like a mandala to me, focusing my mind and my energy so that everything else in the universe was blocked out of consciousness. When I meditated on her, it felt like things were starting to make sense. I felt less confused and more focused on something that seemed, somehow, important. Her flame-red hair, torn clothing and boots, adorned a body that instantly ignited my desires whenever I looked at her, and yet it was her thoughts, her way of talking, and her mind itself that were the most fascinating and exciting things about her to me.

While Colleen was both angry and unhappy with the world, she also possessed an unusual capacity for optimism, which was expressed in her idealistic belief that the world we lived in could be improved. She was unique among my teenage friends in that she believed she had the power to initiate this change. While I felt myself swept along in the unending cycles of Being, impotent to make any real or lasting change to the order of things, Colleen seemed confident that she could assert her will stridently enough to alter the course of history.

"The things you do to change the world don't have to be monumental or epic," she said as we walked. "I want to feed the hungry that live in our community and work with the homeless. I want to lessen the suffering that I see around me, little by little. That would make me feel like I've done something."

"But there will always be hungry and homeless people. And the reason that they will always exist is because of the system that we all live in. Working with a few starving and homeless people is like putting a band-aid on the problem. I think the system itself has to be destroyed before things get better."

Colleen looked exasperated. "So you're not willing to do anything until you can solve everything? That's no solution at all! How do you know that destroying this system is going to make anything better? I bet, in fact, that things would become a lot worse if there was a revolution. Yes, this system does promote a lot of suffering and pain, but so does any system. Suffering and pain will exist no matter what system you live under, whether it be democracy or anarchy. I think it makes a lot more sense to act in the here and now, and try to help who we can with what we have. There is no utopia; only concrete individuals who suffer and die. Let's try and help make life for them a bit less awful."

I understood and was sympathetic with her point, but I was also too invested in my own image of myself to admit this to Colleen.

VI.

"Punk rock! Suck my cock!" a group of teenage boys yelled out the window of a passing car. The faces were familiar. They were members of the local high school football team with whom we regularly had trouble.

"Fuck you, you fuckin' jocks!" Colleen and I yelled in defiance.

This time our response elicited only laughs from our tormentors, and they continued driving down the road, disappearing in the distance. At another time, the car might have stopped, and we would have been faced with a physical confrontation. Sometimes these confrontations would end in humiliation; sometimes they would end in triumph. They were an ongoing part of our teenage years.

Teenage life is filled with fiery passion of all sorts.

VII.

The club was crammed with bodies, all swaying and moving to the sounds of the band on stage. This was not the place to talk or to fight, but to feel unified with others. We were all crushed together, flowing like tides in a body of water that was reacting to the guitar chords and the drumbeats of the performers. Colleen and I stood shoulder-to-shoulder, singing along with the lyrics, pumping our fists in the air and periodically turning to one another and laughing. It felt like time had stopped and that we were simply existing in an eternal sea that was lap, lap, lapping against the walls of the nightclub.

"Hey you fuckin' guys!"

I felt a shove from behind and turned to see our friend Kendrick looming at our backs. The glazed look on his face told me that he was in an altered state of consciousness. His arms extended to embrace both Colleen and I at once, hugging us tightly and drawing us all together so close that it felt like we had become one unified being. I felt his beard stubble rub against my cheek and the sweat from his face smear against my forehead. I could smell his damp, salty body. He kissed me on the eye and then he kissed Colleen on the forehead.

"You are wonderful! Heaven-sent!" he said, not yelling, but vocalizing loud enough that we could hear him above the music. "You look amazing! Wonderful!" This emanated from him like an ecstatic moan; a vocal orgasm. We pulled away from him but he wouldn't let go, insistently engulfing us once again in his arms and holding us against his body.

Colleen and I exchanged looks with one another and laughed. The band finished the song they had been playing and began another. When Kendrick heard this, his arms flew into the air, releasing us from his grip. He gave a loud "Whoop!" and started to bounce up and down, moving away from us and through the crowd toward the stage.

"He's definitely on something!" The voice boomed from my left. I turned to see our friend Richard standing next to me, positioned so that he could talk directly into my ear. He pulled back, smiling and gave a short laugh that made his shoulders and arms move up and down, like he was going through a slight convulsion.

"Yeah, I think so." I laughed as a guy with a bright blue mohawk pushed past us, disappearing into the dark crowd of people.

VIII.

The music reached a pace and a pitch that made all attempts to resist jumping into the pit impossible.

"We are One! We are One! We are One!

They can't keep us down,
No matter how they try.
You can see us in your town,
Hear our battle cry!

We are One! We are One! We are One!"

"The pit" was the swirl of bodies rotating and slamming into one another like a whirlpool in front of the stage. Periodically the flow would be broken when someone fell to the floor or when someone leapt from the stage into the midst of the turning bodies. On these occasions, the dancers would come together either to help the fallen get back to their feet, or to catch the person descending from the air. Afterwards the flow of bodies would continue their circular journey, once again creating a whirlpool of movement.

As if caught in the slipstream of the guy with the blue mohawk, Colleen, Richard and I rushed into the pit and were swept into its rotations. Elbows high, marching forward, at each moment I was unsure of whether it was my own power that was moving me or whether I was being carried by the rest of the dancers. Images blurred through my field of view; shaven heads, colored hair, spikes, leather jackets and chains. Occasionally I would get a glimpse of the people in the band; the singer bellowing his lyrics, the guitarist intent and focused on his instrument. There were no distinct sounds, only a disembodied roar permeating the organism of which we were all parts. The music, the voices, the clapping and the stomping converged. I was no longer conscious of where I was or what I was doing. Drenched in sweat, I pressed into the group and became a functioning part of the whole.

"We are One! We are One! We are One!"

IX.

When the show came to an end we found Kendrick lip-locked in the arms of a girl with green spiked hair who was wearing a Charles Manson t-shirt.

"Hey," he said, reluctantly pulling away from his new friend. "Can we get a ride? I'm going to stay over at Sienna's place." He nodded toward the girl, his eyes squinty and his mouth formed into a grin. The girl smiled as well, though surprisingly her expression appeared not to be clouded by the effects of intoxicants.

"Sure. Where do you live?" I asked the girl.

"Not far. Just about 15 minutes."

We all loaded into my car. I was driving the Cutlass, which was big enough to hold about eight people if they didn't mind being crushed together. Kendrick and Sienna hopped into the back seat, still groping one another and joined at the mouths.

As we drove, I kept asking for directions from Ms. Manson, but she was more interested in the exchange of bodily fluids than in the practical task of helping me navigate toward the unknown destination where I was to drop her and Kendrick. Each time that I interrupted their make-out session for further directions, she looked exasperated and became increasingly impatient with me until the point at which I myself got fed-up.

"Look! Do you want me to drop you right fuckin' here?!" I finally exploded, jamming on the brakes and stopping the car in the middle of the street. When I glared at Sienna in the rear-view mirror, I expected some sort of apology, but instead what I saw was an expression of pure hostility engraved on her face. As my gaze locked with her's, she slowly, deliberately – but silently – mouthed the words, "I - will - kill-you."

My heart beat faster, and my pulse raced. This girl was nuts. As I continued to stare at her, she continued to wear that angry expression of defiance before abruptly changing her facial expression and swapping it for the same blank smile she had worn in the club. This change occurred just as Colleen turned around to see what she was doing.

"Oh. I'm just around the corner," Sienna said, looking at Colleen with that fake grin.

Unsettled and a bit scared, I followed her directions and stopped in front of a three storey apartment building. Kendrick and Sienna got out of the car and, after using a key to get in the gate, disappeared up the stairs.

"That chick is psycho," I said to Colleen. "I'm worried."

Colleen looked at me with concern.

"I think we should go up there and make sure Kendrick's OK."

Colleen and I quickly got out of the car and approached the security gate behind which Kendrick and the girl had disappeared. It was locked, so we started to press the buttons on the wall next to the entryway hoping that someone would buzz us in. Almost immediately, there was a rattling, metal-on-metal noise signaling that one of the residents upstairs had remotely unlocked the gate, and so we slipped in and up the stairs. We got in just fast enough to see Kendrick and the girl as they entered an apartment on the second floor, shutting the door behind them. We went up and tried the knob. It was unlocked.

When we let ourselves into the apartment, Kendrick turned

around, surprised. He smiled, exclaiming, "What are you guys doing here!"

I looked around the room. The walls were blank, and the only piece of furniture that I could see was a bookcase filled with paperbacks. Other than that, the apartment was bare, its white walls unmarred by any sorts of markings or ornamentation, as if the place was vacant. This gave me the creeps.

"I need to use the bathroom," I said, just as Sienna, looking angry, came out of an adjoining room; the kitchen I think.

Colleen wandered over to the bookcase and started to scan the shelves as I approached what I surmised to be the bathroom. I heard Sienna yell, "Wait a minute!" but I was already pulling the cord for the light by the time she ran up to me and grabbed my arm. As the bulb flickered on, I saw a room as empty as the rest of the apartment. There were no toiletries; no toothbrush, no soap, no towels. Nothing. Everything was white: the tub, the sink, the walls, the floor, the toilet. Everything, that is, except for a vividly obvious spray of red liquid spreading across the back of the toilet, onto the ring of the seat and into the bowl. There was enough of this crimson fluid that it dripped bit by bit, plopping into the unflushed water, dribbling from a largish pool formed near the seat's hinges. The contrast seemed purposely staged for dramatic effect, like a scene from an art film. Red against white. Sterility versus contamination. If I had been more emotionally detached, I might have been able to appreciate the aesthetics, but instead, my heart began to race, and I felt a burning flood of stomach acid rush into my throat. Reflexively, I recoiled, retreating from the bathroom and back into the hallway, almost knocking Sienna over, as she was still grasping onto my arm.

"What the fuck is wrong with you?!" She yelled, as she nearly toppled to the ground.

"What the fuck is wrong with you?!" I replied, pointing to the toilet.

"Fuck you! I had my period! This is my place not yours!"

Colleen appeared and shoved Sienna out of the way. "C'mon. Let's go," she said grabbing my arm and pulling me toward the door.

"Kendrick!" I yelled. "You better come with us!"

Kendrick looked confused, but he followed us out of the apartment as if on reflex.

There was a fire extinguisher in a glass case along the stairs, and as I passed it, I smashed the glass with my elbow, grabbed the canister, activated it by pulling the pin blocking its trigger and then started spraying white clouds of fire retardant up the stairs. I could lie and say that this was an instinctive attempt to impede an attack from Sienna in case she decided to follow us. However, at the time there was no such calculation on my part. I simply felt like I wanted to cause a bit of havoc. I had seen blood. I had been made to feel fearful. I just wanted to spread the bad feelings around and instill some terror in this girl.

Once on the street we pushed Kendrick into the car and I sped off, screeching the tires and giving the Cutlass's 350 cubic inch V-8 engine an opportunity to prove its capacity to produce a tremendous amount of torque. It was a great get-away vehicle. I popped a couple of antacid tablets once we were a safe distance from the scene, extinguishing the horrendous heartburn creeping up my esophagus.

"What the fuck was that all about!?" Kendrick asked as we sped down the city street. He was laughing, obviously not all that upset.

"She's a fuckin' psycho, Kendrick!" Colleen yelled. "Look at her diary!"

Colleen had swiped one of the volumes shelved on Sienna's bookcase and was now holding it open to a page inscribed with a childish looking drawing of a male figure whose penis had apparently been amputated by a female figure standing next to him. The female figure held a knife in one hand and the penis in her other hand. She looked suspiciously like Sienna.

"It was on the bookcase!" Colleen yelled at Kendrick, shoving the open pages in his face. "She fuckin' filled it with cartoon drawings of naked, mutilated men covered in blood. That's all that's in it. Nothing else."

Kendrick wasn't laughing any more.

As we continued to make our getaway from Sienna's apartment, Colleen pulled the diary away from Kendrick's face and continued to leaf through its pages.

" Every single page," she muttered. "And under each of the drawings she scrawled, 'I AM PUSSYWHIP.' What a fuckin' psycho!"

X.

Passion, like fire, can be both beneficial and hazardous. Sometimes one needs to risk the hazards in order to reap the benefits. At other times, the benefits are just not worth the costs.

CHAPTER FOUR: SPACE

I.

Passionate teenagers may potentially grow to be passionate adults as long as the world's influences don't succeed in extinguishing all youthful inner fire. Young passion can be channeled and harnessed, eventually to become a well of motivation that energizes and enhances life. More often, however, the world slowly wears down the young, encouraging them to forget that everything is possible; that nothing is established once and for all. When this happens, passionate youngsters become fearful adults who, in recoiling from the dark void of freedom, look to others for salvation. That's when they willingly consent to become cogs in a machine.

II.

I chose to pursue philosophy as a career because I was passionate about the subject, not because I expected to become rich, famous or to gain a great deal of respect. Philosophy is not a subject that has ever been in high popular demand, and so those of us who do find employment in the field are normally quite willing to work under whatever conditions are offered. One of the conditions I found consistently in place at most of the institutions where I was employed was the requirement that I be shoehorned into an office housing at least one other person. It was rare that I ever had a space of my own.

My office mates were not always, nor were they usually, fellow philosophers. I have shared space with English teachers, Spanish teachers, history teachers as well as philosophy teachers. Such arrangements are not necessarily unpleasant, but I did start to develop the feeling that my presence was more of an afterthought than a necessity. Part-time or temporary philosophy instructors come and go, and they can be made to fit in anywhere. It's not practical to set aside a unique space in which they do their work and which they alone use. Better then for such individuals to make their accommodations wherever, and whenever, there is space available.

This sort of attitude produced a very definite effect in me. I came to feel as if my duties were not perceived as important in themselves, but only in relation to the changing conditions and needs of the institution. This was strange because to me, personally, philosophy was the most important discipline of all, and yet those around me treated it like an ornament; something that was nice to have available but not necessary when you got right down to it. In the modern educational environment, the oldest academic discipline of them all had become an anachronism and I, as a philosopher, a mere curiosity.

III.

My first teaching job was a part-time assignment teaching two sections of logic at a small, rural community college. The position required that I commute 90 miles from home three times a week. I was young, and having just finished graduate school, eager to get started working as a philosopher. I was ready to accept any position that would give me some experience to fill out my resume and to pursue my passion.

When I was hired, I was informed that I would share an office with Dr. Jacob Allin.

Jacob was an asshole, but I eventually came to like him. When

I first met him he was complaining about how much work he had to do and how bad he was at his job. He was a philosophy teacher, and he claimed that he hated teaching.

"Why did you study philosophy then?" I asked.

"Because I wanted to philosophize. I never wanted to deal with all of these bellyaching students. I don't think that most people who study philosophy really want to teach. They want to discover the meaning of life, or something like that."

It seemed natural, so I asked, "Have you discovered the meaning of life?"

"Yes," he answered, not at all hesitant.

"What is it?" I asked, smirking.

"Well, it's like I tell my students. There is no meaning in life. It's all meaningless. I figure that the only way to give your life some kind of direction is to piss as many people off as you can. I take that to heart as a teacher. If I upset my students, preferably to the point of depression, then I've earned my paycheck."

Jacob let out a laugh. It was a laugh that meant something, so I knew right away that he was not being completely sincere with me.

Jacob considered himself to be a cynic; not necessarily in the original sense of the ancient Greeks, but in the more common, popular sense. He claimed that all people lie to themselves and that they will continue to lie to themselves even when shown the truth. Most people, in addition, are stupid and can't be taught. They are led by convention, satisfied with superficialities, and hate change. The only reason to associate with other people, he claimed, was to confront them with their own idiocy.

"I really don't like people too much," he laughed in what sounded like a good natured way.

"What about your wife?" I asked. "Don't you like her?"

"She's OK."

He laughed once again and I saw that he was guilty of the

same sins that he saw in others. He wasn't being honest with me or with himself. Our conversation was a superficial diversion to take his mind off of other matters. His "cynicism" was a convenient and simple way to deal with the complications of the world. It was his device for navigating through the uncomfortable terrain of human interaction. When he had to confront a serious topic, he would adopt an attitude of cynical superiority and thereby avoid any of the annoying complexities and possible errors that the "naive" would encounter. He could be certain at every step of his life that he possessed wisdom by virtue of his privileged position of cynical "objectivity." By taking nothing and no one seriously, Jacob insulated himself from the world, other people and himself.

IV.

Jacob was certain that he had cancer. I asked him if he had been to the doctor to be examined.

"No," he said.

"What makes you think you have cancer?" I asked.

"Oh, there's no real reason except that it seems like the kind of thing that would happen to me. I'm destined to die of some painful and horrible disease."

I did not like Jacob when I first met him. He embodied all of the things that I hated in my worst college professors. I witnessed his interactions with some of his students and was struck by how easily he dismissed their concerns and how superior he acted toward them. He took nothing too seriously because it seemed that he took nothing seriously at all. Over the course of the year, however, my opinion of Jacob began to change. The more that I conversed with him, the more I realized that his cynicism was not the result of meanness or arrogance but was a symptom of his weak and defeated feelings about his own life.

"I've never felt like I accomplished all of the things that I should have over the course of my career," he once confided. "Did you know that before studying philosophy I was an artist? I can't wait until I'm up for retirement so that I can go back to painting. That's where my real passion lies."

This admission encouraged me to rethink my conclusions about Jacob. I no longer thought of him simply as an asshole, but as a vulnerable and sad man. It is impossible to feel sympathy for someone who you think is constantly looking down on you, and I began to realize that Jacob was looking down not at me or his students, but down upon himself. This realization allowed me to first feel pity and then sympathy for him. It also seemed to create a change in the way that we interacted with one another. As I warmed to Jacob, he seemed to warm up to me, the cynical facade disappearing in the process. We began to have short, serious conversations about our life goals and about our personal strengths and weaknesses. He began to give me worthwhile advice concerning my career and put to rest some of the long held worries I harbored about pursuing philosophy professionally. It turned out that Jacob didn't really hate teaching at all, but loved it so much that he could not stand those who were not serious about philosophy. He truly desired for his students and peers to achieve their full potentials, and when they didn't do so he became frustrated. You might say that he hated people so much because he loved them so much.

"You know," Jacob said to me one day, "There's nothing more noble than a weak man who strives to be strong. But there's also nothing more pathetic than a strong man who strives to be weak."

Jacob, it turned out, did have cancer. His wife coaxed him to go to see a doctor after he began to experience some especially severe headaches. An inoperable tumor was discovered in his brain and he died within a month.

V.

Without space, there would be nothing else. All things depend upon the openness of space in order to have a place in which to be. The classroom, for instance, is not simply the walls, nor the ceiling, nor the floor; it is the space in between the walls, the ceiling and the floor in which the drama of a class unfolds.

An office, likewise, is more than just a room. It is a space where one can interact with colleagues, repose, conduct conferences, write, grade papers, fill out forms, think, be depressed. Sharing office space with another person requires compromise, but it also forces interaction. It is a space in which life worlds come to overlap with one another. Just as in the classroom, it is a place where dramas unfold.

VI.

When I finally landed a job as a full-time philosophy teacher, I was not only relieved to finally have achieved some degree of career stability, I was also unusually pleased to find that I was granted an office of my own. Here, instead of bare, unornamented walls and an empty desk, there were books and photos, posters and busts that I chose and that I enjoyed looking at. Finally, I felt as if I could build my own private enclave in which I was a dweller rather than an intruder. Having my own office space, where I could leave my belongings and know that they were secure, where I could open the door and not worry that I would be disturbing someone else, and where I could sit without being disturbed, created a new sort of situation for me. It allowed me to be fully present with my work and with students. With a permanent job and my own office, I felt more secure and my surroundings felt more predictable and stable. I felt more at home. I didn't feel like an intruder or an interloper. I was at home in a place that I occupied fully.

I had been a student at this very same college when I was younger. It was where Colleen and I first met. Little did I know that the office I now occupied had previously been the office of one of our teachers.

"Did you know that there is an unusual history to your office space?" It was the chairman of the department who said this to me.

"An unusual history?" I repeated. "What history is that?"

"Years ago, your office was occupied by one of our English professors. He ended up losing his mind. It's kind of a campus legend."

The chairman paused for an extended period of time and looked at me smiling. His smile, combined with his silence, seemed to be intended as subtly dramatic, and perhaps ominous. It was like he was letting me in on a dirty secret. In doing so, it felt like he was trying to demonstrate to me that I was being trusted with information that would initiate me into becoming a full member of the campus community. I was on the inside now.

"Dr. Spengler was one our oldest faulty members."

"I took a class from him when I was a student here!" I exclaimed upon hearing Spengler's name. "I couldn't stand the man. Every day in class he would berate us all, telling us how stupid we were and how we would never amount to anything."

The chairman let out a bit of a laugh.

"That doesn't surprise me. Over the years he became more and more unstable. You probably had a class with him just before his final breakdown.

When he first started here at the college he was one of our most popular English professors. The students loved him and the other members of the faculty thought he was brilliant. But, you know, there was always something about him that seemed a bit unhinged. Maybe that's part of what people liked about him. He was quirky; a little paranoid, but in a funny, charming kind of way. Over the years his paranoia became amplified. It got to the point where it became scary rather than funny. That's when his troubles really began.

He abandoned his wife. He was certain that she was plotting against him somehow, and so he moved out of their house and started living in his office; what is now your office. He had one of those big, cardboard moving wardrobes in the corner, and used it as his closet. He slept on the floor and ate at local restaurants. He took showers at the gym. He never let the janitors into his office, insisting that no one had the right to violate the sanctity of his space.

The administration got wind of what was going on, but they let it slide. Spengler was well liked and respected. I guess the idea was that he was a harmless eccentric who was otherwise a contributing member of the college community. So for about a year he lived in his office undisturbed.

People became more concerned, however, when they started to see him sunbathing out on the roof wearing only his underwear. When the guy that was our chairman at the time confronted him about this, Spengler got very angry. He yelled, 'Don't you tell me how to behave in MY house!' At this point it seemed like things were getting out of hand. But no one wanted to do anything. I guess everyone just hoped that his behavior would reach a point where it sort of stabilized and didn't get any worse.

Well, that's not what ended up happening. Before too long a young girl brought charges against him for sexual harassment. It seems that Spengler grabbed her and tried to kiss her when she came to visit him during his office hours. She was traumatized by the event, but Spengler insisted that it was the young woman who had made a pass at him. Of course no one believed this; he was crazy, 70 years old and quite an awful sight. Even his own wife wanted nothing to do with him.

The case went to court and Spengler was found to be incompetent. The young woman could have brought charges against the school, but she ended up dropping the case altogether. It wasn't too long after that Spengler was found drowned in the lake on the south end of the campus. No one knows if it was suicide, an accident or murder.

In any case; there you have it. Your office is quite the campus landmark."

VII.

As I sat in my office and looked around, I kept thinking about how this was where Spengler lived for that year of insanity. While I was sitting in his English class, being subjected to his abusive tirades, he was living his horrible life, the details of which I was not aware. As a student I thought he was just a mean old man. In reality he was a miserable, tortured lunatic.

At the time I was a student I couldn't know that I would occupy this man's office space many years in the future. Now that I am sitting here, in my chair, at my desk, looking at the walls, the ceiling and the floor, I think how it was in this very space that Spengler wrestled with his illness. It was here that he assaulted a student. When I was socializing with my friends, riding my motorcycle, or listening to music, Spengler's own life was unfolding as well. Our worlds intersected in the classroom and now, years later, they have intersected here in this office once again.

No doubt there have been many, many other people who used this office space over the course of the years. I suppose that somewhere there must be a record of who these people were, what positions they held, how long they were employed, how much they were paid, and on and on. My name is, of course, among the litany, and some day in the future there may be some other philosophy, or English, or history professor who will settle into this same space and wonder about who it was that held office hours here and what sorts of dramas played out. They might even hear stories from some of their elder colleagues about me and how strange, or friendly, or depressed, or how weird I was. They might be told about how it was that I eventually died. Maybe they'll try to imagine what I was like and then think a bit about how they themselves are destined to work, grow old and die as well.

VIII.

At first I did not recognize the student waiting outside of my office. She stood there, in the open doorway, clutching a stack of books to her chest with one arm while rapping the knuckles of her other hand against the open door.

"Hi," she said. "Can I talk with you about my grade from last semester?"

This was a common thing. Every semester I teach five to six classes with an average enrollment of 30 to 40 students per class. With hundreds of students cycling through the classes, it is nearly impossible to remember each and every person; especially when, as happens every semester, some of those students rarely show up to class meetings. In the case of the young woman at the door, I could vaguely remember her presence in one of last semester's classes, but I could not immediately pin down which one.

"Come in and sit down. Which class were you in?" I said, pointing to an empty chair near my desk.

The young woman frowned and gave off an air of annoyance. "I was in your Introduction to Philosophy class. My name is Marlene."

"OK Marlene. Let me get my gradebook out and I can go over your records."

I removed the last semester's gradebook from my file cabinet, set it down on my desk, and then turned to the section for Introduction to Philosophy.

"Now, what is your last name?" I asked.

Again, Marlene looked annoyed. "Lavine," she said.

I scanned the three separate sections in my records for the previous semester's Introduction to Philosophy classes. In the last of these sections I found the name Marlene Lavine. Her final score for the class was 113 out of 200 points, which translated into a final grade of F.

"OK," I said, looking up toward the student. "So what is it that you wanted to talk about?"

"Well, you gave me an F. I don't understand why it is that you failed me in the class."

I smiled. "Well, let's take a look."

I ran my finger across the row of scores that appeared by her name and read them out one by one.

"There were 50 points allotted for attendance and participation. It looks like you attended less than half of the classes, so you earned 23 points for that portion of your grade. You did not take three of the four quizzes that I assigned. You did take quiz number 3, on which you scored 10 points, so your overall quiz total is 10 out of 50. You did well on your midterm paper, scoring 45 out of 50, but on your final paper you scored only 35 out of 50. Your total score for the class, then, adds up to 113 points out of a possible 200 points."

"So why did I fail the class?" the student asked again.

I smiled at Marlene again, trying to muster my patience. I also started to feel a burning sensation creep from my stomach up into my esophagus. My heartburn was starting to erupt once again.

"Your final score is below 60% of the points possible. If you review your syllabus, you'll find that on the grading scale this earns you an F for the class."

Marlene looked angry.

"I don't think that's fair. I did a good job on the midterm."

"Yes you did," I agreed. "However, the midterm is only one of the required assignments. Again, if you review your syllabus, you'll see that your final grade is calculated on the basis of the four criteria I just went over with you: attendance, quizzes, midterm, and final."

"Well, I never got a syllabus; and I don't see why attendance should count so much."

I'm sure that Marlene was not aware that I had been through this many times with many students in the past. Nonetheless, every time that this did happen, my heart would start to beat a bit faster, my breathing would start to get a bit shallower and my heartburn would become more and more intense. This was a sign to me that my patience was running out and that I was teetering on the edge of losing my temper.

"Marlene, I handed the syllabus out on the first day of class. I also posted it on the class website. You could have asked for a copy at any time during the semester."

Marlene launched into an explanation for her lack of participation in the class. "I was very busy last semester with personal stuff. I haven't been feeling well and my mom has been out of work so I've had a hard time dealing with her issues. Besides that, my sister is a total bitch, and she hasn't been supportive of my mom, so it has been totally my responsibility to keep the house in order. So you can see, I just didn't have time to come to class or do all of the assignments. I mean, there's more to life than school after all!" Marlene looked at me slack jawed and exasperated.

"I understand," I said, making a conscious effort to sound patient and to explicitly affirm Marlene's difficulties. "Family matters are important, and they do get in the way of other things sometimes. I can see why you were distracted from your schoolwork last semester and were not able to do well in the class."

The angry expression on Marlene's face became intensified. "Will you change my grade then?"

My pulse spiked and a surge of hot stomach acid rose into my throat. I gagged for a moment and covered my mouth with my fist. Swallowing hard, I winced and then, speaking through my fist as if it was megaphone, said, "No, I won't change your grade."

Marlene stared at me, aware that I was in discomfort, but not at all concerned. "Can't I just do some extra work for a few more points so that I can pass the class? I need this class in order to transfer to the school that I'm going to next year. If I don't pass this class they won't let me attend."

"No. I can't do that. The requirements for the class were clearly outlined at the start of the semester. In future, make sure that you know what is expected of you when you enroll in a class."

I wanted to launch into a lecture. I wanted to tell Marlene that doing well in philosophy class is not just a matter of getting a few extra points, but of demonstrating an understanding of philosophical thinking and of showing a willingness to linger with some of the most important questions that human beings have ever asked themselves. Philosophy is not separate from life; it is part of life. It is not something to just get through so that you can get on with other things. It is an end in itself.

I knew that Marlene was not interested in hearing any of this however. All she wanted was a passing grade. And all I wanted was for her to leave my office and for this awful heartburn to subside.

IX.

When Walter first came to my office, he said it was in order to get feedback on a paper he was writing. He sat in the empty chair next to my desk and I read through his rough draft.

The topic I had asked students to write about concerned the issue of suffering in life. We had been studying the Hellenistic philosophers, many of whom offered ideas and strategies for dealing with feelings of despair, and so for the midterm paper I asked students to describe a time in their own lives when they had struggled with depression and to discuss how the suggestions of the Cynics, Stoics or Epicureans might apply to their own experience.

Walter was a quiet student who rarely spoke in class, and yet it was apparent from his demeanor and comportment that he was fully engaged with the material we were studying. He was never absent from class and was always fully alert and attentive to what was being discussed. When he did speak, his comments were clearly formulated and on point. More important than this, however, was the fact that Walter exuded seriousness and a sort of care for the subject matter that is hard to quantify. As I sat there in my office, reading the rough draft of his midterm paper, I came to better understand why it was that Walter was so interested in what we were studying.

Walter's paper was a chronicle of personal suffering, the degree of which I could hardly imagine. When he was 14, his mother died of cancer and when he was 17, his father committed suicide. Walter explained how his feelings of abandonment and loss led him, on the one hand, to pursue stability in life by settling into a career as a motorcycle mechanic, but on the other hand he was also led to quiet his despair by becoming addicted to drugs and alcohol. What he wanted most was a life that was predictable and relationships that were stable, and yet he consistently found himself entangled in love affairs with women who cheated on him and friendships with men who betrayed him.

Walter wrote that there was no great, dramatic event leading him to realize he was suffering and unhappy. Rather, he felt as if he was on a "slow boil," which manifested itself in a chronic and persistent feeling of anxiety and discontent. At the age of 20, he decided to go back to college, not in order to pursue a particular degree program or career path, but in order to study and learn about the great thinkers of the world, and to see if their wisdom was of any use in helping him discover the meaning of life.

Upon reading about the Cynics, Stoics and Epicureans, Walter explained that he felt at home. For the first time, he had discovered individuals who gave expression to the sorts of thoughts that he himself had been struggling with for many, many years. In particular, he resonated with the Cynic Diogenes, who offered a diagnosis and a cure for human suffering. According to Diogenes, we suffer when we strive toward goals that are unattainable. Society encourages us to pursue things like wealth, power and prestige, but what we inevitably find is that the desire for these things is unquenchable. We can never get enough money or fame or influence because these desires have no natural boundaries. Unlike the satisfaction we gain from simple, natural pleasures like eating and sleeping, the unnatural pleasures are limitless, and thus vain. Whereas our bodies naturally tell us when our stomachs are full or when we have had enough sleep, if we commit ourselves to the pursuit of money or fame or prestige, we find that there are no natural indications for when enough is enough. People make themselves anxious, depressed and unhappy chasing after such goals, and so Diogenes counseled his students to give up on the unnatural pleasures and to live a simple life pursuing only those natural pleasures that truly make us happy.

Walter explained that the lesson he learned for his own life by reading about Diogenes was not so much that he should simply "eat, drink and be happy," but that he needed to realize how, since the death of his mother, and especially since the death of his father, he had been trying to replace them with other people and with drugs and alcohol. The stability of his family had been taken away from him, and so he had been trying to surround himself with distractions that would allow him to forget what was really at the core of his anxiety and despair. But the attempt to replace his mother and father was in vain; they could never be replaced. Simply coming to terms with this fact, Walter confessed, was enormously important for him, and though it brought him a great deal of anguish, he hoped that it would open the door to a path that was more edifying than the one he currently found himself walking.

X.

My office is a room with four walls, a ceiling and a floor. Its contents are arranged neatly. There are books on the shelves, pictures and diplomas on the wall. There is a computer sitting on the desk. Next to the desk is a filing cabinet and a paper shredder.

But there is much more here that you can't see.

CHAPTER FIVE: TIME

I.

Each semester passed into the next. One year passed into another. I encountered so many students over the course of my employment at the college that their faces and names became indistinct and lost amidst other vague memories from the past, such as the particular food I ate for breakfast on a certain morning, or the exact amount of money that I paid to fill the tank of my car one afternoon on my way home from work.

I hated this. Students, real human beings with whom I shared philosophical conversations, were forgotten and reduced to insignificant details on the path of my career.

Philosophy had become a job.

II.

The passage of time was a complicated, strange and bifurcated experience for me. In the long-run, on the scale of years, time seemed to rush by quickly. As my tenure review approached, it was difficult for me to believe that I had already been at the college for 5 years. I still felt like a new-comer, an outsider to the culture of the campus community.

On the small scale, the scale of days and hours, time dragged by slowly. Each morning that I arrived on campus, the day felt like it would go on forever. There were classes to conduct, students to meet with, conferences to attend and papers to grade. It felt like the work would never come to an end.

Moments felt like years and years felt like moments.

When I was young, this experience was exactly reversed. At 20, it felt to me as if the years were dragging on into eternity while the hours of each day slipped endlessly into nothingness. The moments of each day flew by too quickly, and when I measured them against the expanse of time that lay ahead of me in life, it seemed as if I had forever to go nowhere in particular. I was wandering about with no direction or purpose. I existed in the moment, and the moment had no meaning or significance without the direction offered by a long-term goal. I knew something had to change.

At that time, I lived with a number of friends in a squalid flat, playing in a punk-rock band, working behind the counter at a movie theatre and taking occasional classes at the very college at which I am now a professor. I longed for my existence to develop some sort of cohesiveness, some sort of purpose that would unify all of my seemingly unrelated activities and interests. Without such an overarching purpose I was aimless, and so I made a decision. I formulated a number of life goals that I wanted to pursue. At the time of their formulation, these objectives seemed important and valuable in themselves. I anticipated that if I was to accomplish even a few of them, I would be deeply satisfied and happy with myself. At the age of 20, then, I embarked on what I believed would be a path to building a contented life.

The formulation of long-term goals forced me to think outside of the moment and to anticipate the future. Daily, I trained myself to see everything through the lens of my overarching objectives, thus transforming each seemingly disconnected and fragmentary moment into an instrument useful for the completion of my goals. In this fashion I moved forward, always anticipating how every minute, every hour, every day, every month and every year would contribute

to my overall plan. Nothing was a waste, I decided. Everything I
did was focused on the future, my future. Everything I did would be
consolidated within the project that was my life.

With this perspective in mind, I enrolled in graduate school
and earned a Ph.D. I published a book and I struggled to secure a
position at a college teaching philosophy. In the process of pursuing
these goals, I did, for a period, overcome my aimlessness. In developing
the habit of looking past the moment, I became adept at putting even
the most mundane details of my life into a meaningful perspective. It all
made sense for a while.

Now, here I am in an ironic situation. I have worked all this
time, starting when I was 20, to accomplish the few goals that were
important to me. At the age of 44 I have completed my doctorate,
I have published the book I longed to write and I have found a
secure position teaching philosophy. But now that these goals have
been accomplished, I am without purpose once again. Now that the
objectives I have pursued for the last 24 years are in my grasp, they have
lost their value. All along these goals were the carrots that motivated
me to be active, and now that these carrots have been consumed and
digested, the old hunger pains have resurfaced, accompanied by a
persistent and uncomfortable indigestion.

When I lived in the moment, the moments lacked meaning
because they played no role in a larger life project. Now that I have
actualized my life project, I have come to question the worth of the
project itself. This seems to be the root of my strange experience of
time. When I operated without a goal, I was not encouraged to think
about the future and consequently the moments came like random
machinegun fire into an abyss. Each instant flew by quickly, uniquely
and without reason. Once I fixed my sights on a target, the moments
came more slowly and deliberately as I anticipated how efficiently they
would travel toward their destination. Now that I have achieved my
goals, I see everything from the perspective of the end point. Now that

I have arrived at the target, shooting at it seems superfluous.

III.

I hear lots of people saying that the greatest happiness in life comes from living in the moment. For me, that is a lie. The moment without a future goal is meaningless.

I hear lots of people saying that success and achieving your goals brings happiness. That too is a lie for me. Once achieved, a goal becomes an inert burden. It lacks a future.

The only meaning I've found exists somewhere between the present moment and the future goal.

No moment is intrinsically valuable, nor is any goal. The moment is only valuable insofar as it conveys you toward a goal, and the goal is only valuable insofar as it beckons you to take advantage of the moment.

IV.

Arthur Schopenhauer taught that there are no creatures in the universe that suffer to the same degree as human beings. Our intense suffering, he observed, comes from our capacity to experience time.

Rocks and plants lack the capacity to suffer precisely because they are incapable of thought. A rock simply is what it is. It doesn't aspire toward goals, it doesn't fear the future, and it doesn't worry about the past. It doesn't even make sense to say that a rock exists in the present, since for a rock there is no such thing as time at all. A concept like "the present" only makes sense when considered in relation to "the past" and "the future." Rocks have no temporal concepts since they lack any concepts whatsoever.

Plants may be more complicated than rocks, but they still don't think outside of themselves, and so they don't suffer in the way that human beings do. A plant unfolds and blossoms by the forces of necessity. It doesn't choose to pursue any particular goals and it most certainly doesn't think about where it came from or why it is here. Like rocks, plants lack concepts, and as a result they are incapable of the sort of suffering that comes from ruminating on the past and worrying about the future.

Animals, unlike rocks and plants, do think. But their thinking process is not the same as that of humans. Animals live preoccupied with short-term concerns focused on pleasure, pain and physical survival. An animal recoils from painful stimuli and is attracted to pleasurable stimuli. Thus they learn to avoid dangers and to seek out rewards as they navigate through the world. Time exists for animals, but their focus is practical and concrete. When a danger retreats, animals cease their worries. When a danger is present, that is the only thing that they are concerned with.

Humans exist in a constant state of anxiety since the experience of time is so unrelenting for us. Human beings are always thinking outside of themselves, projecting into the future and worrying about the past. Each moment of our lives is spent anticipating what will happen next and assessing what happened last. As a result, Schopenhauer tells us, we are never content. As we travel through life, we constantly anticipate where we are heading, what we want to do, and what goals and aspirations we should be pursuing. This causes us anxiety. Once we achieve our goals and realize our aspirations, we become bored, not happy, and once again feel the compulsion to pursue another set of projects that in the end will also leave us feeling dissatisfied and impatient. For humans, life consists of a nonstop vacillation between anxiety and boredom that only ends when we die.

V.

Life's a bitch and then you die.

VI.

Despite the suffering it brings, our awareness of the passage of time does have at least one very useful and potentially productive consequence: it makes us aware that we are mortal, finite creatures who have a limited period to exist here in the world. This awareness, which Martin Heidegger refers to as our "being-toward-death," colors and conditions everything that we do. Even in our happiest moments, we know that things don't last forever and that there will be a point at which we ourselves will slip into the abyss of nothingness. We all will eventually die, and while this may paralyze some people with anxiety and fear, it may also serve as the spur that coaxes others to get on with the task of doing something – anything – with the short period of life that they do have.

We are temporal beings who came into existence and who will go out of existence. What we do during that in-between period is up to us.

VII.

It was when I was six years old that I first started to really comprehend the inevitability of death. My pet rat had developed cancer, and my mother and I brought it to the Humane Society in order to have it euthanized. That night, after my mother had tucked me into bed, I lay awake thinking about my pet. I was having trouble grasping the fact that my rat friend was gone, once and for all. Why is it, I wondered, that a little, innocent creature should get a disease, suffer physically, and be gone forever? It just didn't make sense.

Lying there in my bed I cried, but the tears accomplished nothing. My pet was not going to come back to life. I told myself this over and over, but each time that I repeated the facts, they just seemed more cruel and awful. There was nothing comforting in this situation; nothing good nor positive.

And then, by a process of inference, my thoughts became even more bleak.

My pet rat had died because he was a living organism. That

means living organisms eventually die. My mother is a living organism.

The conclusion that necessarily followed was too horrible for me to articulate to myself, but that didn't make it any less obvious. Horror gripped me. I couldn't even cry at that point, as I was paralyzed with terror. One day in the future, my own mother would irretrievably vanish, just like my pet rat. How could that be?

And then the final inference struck me: I too am an organism...

VIII.

As the years passed I started to take careful note of details around me and to reflect, one by one, on the passing moments in my life. When I was watching TV with my mother, I would reflect on the fact that some day in the future, this moment would be nothing more than a memory, that my mother would be gone, and that I would be an old man facing death. When I was having fun at a punk rock show, I would try to catalogue the emotions I was experiencing in anticipation of that point when I would be unable to get out of bed because I was dying. When I drank a cup of coffee, I tried to remember all of the subtle sensations, like the bitterness and the burn of the liquid on the tip of my tongue, knowing that there would come a day when I could drink coffee no more. I stupidly imagined that if I collected together enough of these reflections that somehow I would be able to overcome the inevitable. I would have a comprehensive list describing the details of my life that could be relived again and again, which could be written down and preserved for all eternity. This would give me my revenge against death and finitude. My body might die, but not my recollections.

But there are too many details in real life to catalogue them all. Life is always excess. There is always more to the world than can be described, remembered, listed or documented. My attempts to do so made me realize that my fear of future extinction had led to a preoccupation with the past. I fooled myself into thinking that I could stop the flow of time, halt the flux of Being itself, by solidifying my impressions of what had already transpired. But in so doing I sacrificed the creative present; that moment within which the past and the future converge in the "now," producing the unique chance to do something new and unanticipated.

IX.

Anxiety and fear of the end is the furnace powering human creativity. To reach the endpoint of any endeavor is to suffer a symbolic death. One needs to develop skills at deferring the desire for finality or else risk stagnation.

Life is lived in between the past and the future.

X.

There must be no final truths; only burning questions.

Chapter Six: Tenure

I.

The dinner celebration for tenured faculty was held on a Friday evening at a fancy restaurant downtown. I arrived at the same moment as the college president, and the two of us walked into the establishment together.

"Well congratulations! You must be very happy to have been granted tenure." The president smiled as she spoke, patting me on the shoulder.

I smiled back. "Thank you," I said.

We were greeted by a waitress, who guided us to a long table at the back of the restaurant where the rest of our party was located. It looked as if everyone else had been there for quite some time, drinking wine and socializing. As the president and I approached, we were greeted by the crowd. We then awkwardly went through the introductions and the small talk that have to be endured under such circumstances.

There were five faculty members who were granted tenure that year, and part of the ritual of the evening was for the vice president of the college to read out a laundry list of accomplishments for each of us. For the first half hour of the evening congratulations went around the table as we all marveled at one another's achievements. I thought back to a comment uttered by a newly tenured professor from another college at which I used to work. "Now I don't have to do *anything!*" he said after being heaped with praise. Now that I was in his position, that struck me as unusually depressing, and I had to suppress the desire to get up and leave.

II.

As the meal was served, everybody settled into personal conversations; mostly with those people conveniently seated at each elbow. I talked with the dean of my division, who sat to my left, and with a history teacher, who sat to my right. My mind began to wander during the small talk, and I was very self-conscious sitting there engaging in what felt like idle chatter. We had tenure already, after all. What was the purpose of sitting here and talking about it? I kept wondering how long I should remain in place for the sake of politeness.

Then I began thinking about what would happen if I did something completely rude and inappropriate. What would happen, for instance, if I jumped up on the table and systematically spit in the face of each person present? Or what if I jumped up onto the table, pulled down my pants and pissed on the president's plate of fish? What if I yelled at everyone to shut up and then announced my intention to quit my job and join a terrorist organization?

Of course I did none of these things, but rather sat passively in place with a big, stupid smile plastered across my face.

III.

I can't remember exactly how it occurred, but the conversation between the three of us at my end of the table eventually turned toward the subject of religion and the meaning of life. With this turn, things became more immediately interesting, but also unnerving, to me.

"Well, it's obvious that all of the world's troubles begin and end with religion," the history teacher said to me, and I remember being astounded.

"How can you say that?" I asked.

"I say it because if you look at the historical evidence, it's obvious. Every war that has ever been fought has been instigated by religious fanaticism."

"What about the Nazis and the Communists?" I responded. "They were anti-religious, but they nonetheless initiated some of the worst brutality that the world has ever seen."

"But the Nazis and the Communists replaced conventional religion with their own form of totalitarian faith, so in effect they were religious."

I thought about that for a moment and then said, "It seems to me that the most consistent element in all of the wars that have been fought throughout history is government. Whenever there is a war, there is a government. And sometimes, I would say, it is only religion that keeps government from going to war."

The history teacher chuckled a bit. "No. It's religion that is always used in order to justify war."

I became annoyed at what was beginning to sound like simple dogmatism and overgeneralization. "But isn't that the point? Governments *use* religion in order to justify war. If you understand the guiding ideals of most of the world's religions, you are not going to find war and violence included among their highest principles."

"It doesn't matter what they state as their principles," the history teacher responded. "In fact the only purpose that religion serves is to buttress the power of an elite. It always happens that way. The content of religion is a lie. It is a fairy tale used in order to keep the uneducated masses in line. If we were to eliminate religion, we would eliminate a good deal of the irrational nonsense that corrupts human thinking."

I sighed and said, "But if we're to believe that the only authority is worldly authority, what's to keep governments and tyrants from doing whatever they want? With religion, at least there remains a power higher than that of mere human will."

"Reasonable morality is a good enough replacement for religion. If we just use our logic and our natural abilities to think things through rationally, we will develop a moral code that does not need to make reference to God or the supernatural."

As she uttered this last assertion, the history teacher looked very content. She seemed to see herself as incredibly reasonable and down to earth.

I thought for a moment and then spoke. "The thing is, just saying something doesn't make it so. Logic and reason can establish all sorts of contradictory positions. There are logical reasons for claiming that killing is good and logical reasons for claiming that killing is bad. The logical, internal coherence of a system of belief does not guarantee its truthfulness. People can be persecuted and killed in the name of reason just as easily as they can be persecuted and killed in the name of religion."

The history teacher regarded me with a quizzical look. She said nothing, so I continued to speak.

"In terms of survival value, it also seems as if religion is here to stay. It predates science, and it certainly has not died out with the advent of modern times. It has adapted, grown and survived. I would say on that evidence alone we should be led to suspect that religion serves some sort of purpose for human beings."

I continued. "I imagine the purpose served by religion is that it gives people meaning. For the religious person, the world is not just a mass of particles. Rather, the world has significance and importance. For some of us who have been raised on science, sadly, this is not the case. Personally, I envy religious people. I wish I was able to have faith that the universe and my life within it meant something in the grand scheme of things. Making money, working in my career and getting tenure are fine, but there's a point at which I find myself wishing that there was something more."

The history teacher was looking at me intently, a slight smile on her face. I took from this that I was making some sense and that she was not completely hostile to the sentiments I was expressing.

"Do you have any kids?" she asked.

"No. I have a pet cat and a dog." I smiled broadly.

She laughed. "You should have kids. They bring meaning to your life. Religion brings fake meaning, but kids bring real meaning." And that was all she had to say.

IV.

The natural world consists of a realm circumscribed by time and space, and thus it is inherently finite. Religious longing is the longing for infinity, and thus it can never be satisfied by anything within the natural world.

The scientist finds happiness by denying the longing for infinity.

The religious person finds happiness by affirming the existence of a realm beyond time and space.

The nihilist is unable either to deny the longing for infinity or to affirm a realm beyond time and space. Happiness is thus denied to the nihilist and is replaced with endless, vain struggle and hopeless despair. We long for something that will never be, and it makes us sick.

V.

During my argument with the history professor I began to experience that old burning pain in my stomach. At first I attributed it to heartburn brought on by my meal, and so I tried to ignore the unpleasant sensation, distracting myself with conversation.

But as I sat there at the table, debating the meaning of life, religion and government, the discomfort in my stomach intensified, moving into my chest and up my throat. The more that I tried to ignore the feeling, the more intrusive it became, until finally I excused myself and rushed into the bathroom.

VI.

Once in the bathroom, I locked myself in one of the stalls. I sat on the toilet and hung my head between my legs, but as I did this a wave of nausea overcame me and I felt something rise into my throat. Before I was able to stand up and turn around, my mouth filled with stomach acid. The taste and the hot, burning feeling triggered a retching response and I vomited all over my pant legs and my shoes. For a moment I felt a bit better, but then a wave of sickness came over me once again, and once again I threw up a mouthful of reddish brown liquid bile, which was mixed with the contents of the meal I had just consumed.

A puddle of vomit pooled on the floor directly in front of the toilet. I wiped my mouth with tissue paper and sat down once again, trying to relax and to regain my composure. I was sweating profusely.

I heard the bathroom door open and someone walk in. "What's going on in here?" a voice asked.

"I'm not feeling too good. Just give me a minute. I should be fine if you just give me a minute," I called out.

"What are you burning in there? There's no smoking allowed in here," the voice responded.

At first I was confused by this last utterance. I don't smoke, I thought. What is this person talking about? But then I looked at the puddle of vomit on the floor and I realized it was on fire! Wispy tendrils of flame and smoke danced across the surface of the mess, and with that there arose a terrible odor. It was the smell of smoldering stomach acid and partially digested food; this against the vague odor of urine and disinfectant.

Instinctively, I began to stomp out the flames, bringing my foot down repeatedly in the stinking puddle. Vomit splattered all over the walls of the stall, my pant legs and up onto my shirt. The flames went out just as someone began vigorously knocking on the door of the stall. I opened the door, dripping with filth.

"Are you OK?" The man standing in front of me was a waiter. The expression on his face betrayed a mixture of concern and anger.

"I'm not feeling very good," was all that I could say.

VII.

I was able to clean myself up a bit and make a quick escape from the restaurant. Once back home, Colleen greeted me with concern.

"What happened to you?" she asked as I entered the house.

"Stomach problems," I responded. "I started to feel sick and then I threw up. I think maybe I got food poisoning."

"How do you feel now?"

"I'm feeling better. I'm just not cut out for these work functions." I joked.

VIII.

My work routine continued. Day in and day out I conducted classes, discussing issues of deep philosophical significance for a couple of hours before attending meetings and performing the various duties required of tenured members of the college faculty. I now had job security; the very thing I had been after for 24 years.

Despite my job security, a sense of uncertainty continued to gnaw at me. I confided in Colleen that even though objectively everything in our lives was going better than ever, subjectively I felt ill at ease and lacking in self-confidence. After all of these years of study, after decades of hard work, I felt as if I was an ignorant, vulnerable youngster again.

The days came and went; one after the other. There was nothing that I needed to worry about. My relationship with Colleen was as solid as ever. My job was secure. Colleen and I owned our own home. There was no better relationship for me to pursue. There was no better job for me to go after. There was no nicer house to look for.

But because all of these things were set in place, life had taken on a static character. There was a sort of timelessness about my existence insofar as there was nothing challenging to anticipate and nothing threatening to worry about. If I was able to enjoy the moment or to anticipate a better future, then I might be able to avoid thinking about the futility of life in general, and I could be content. However, contentment appeared to be something foreign to my nature. The easier and more placid my life became on the outside, the more unsettled and difficult it became on the inside.

IX.

And my stomach problems continued to get worse. Perhaps I was somaticizing my inner turmoil. Or could it be that my inner turmoil was caused by some physical ailment?

I made an appointment with a doctor in order to investigate.

X.

In his Fire Sermon, The Buddha said, "Everything is burning." The desires of life are like flames that burn and torment us until such a time as we are able to extinguish them and thus experience peace and serenity. In Buddhism, this state of serenity is called *Nirvana*, which means "to snuff out," as in snuffing out a flame. The Buddha taught that if one can snuff out the flames of desire, the suffering of life will also cease.

But I can't see any end to the burning desires of life, except in death. This is why Buddhist serenity eludes me. If, in fact, everything is burning, then to put out the flames and to achieve Nirvana would be to cease existing. It would be to die; to become nothing. And what is more preferable: to suffer or to be nothing?

Chapter Seven: Friends

I.

Over the years that I was focused on establishing my career as a philosopher, I remained close friends with Richard and Kendrick, and I eventually married Colleen. All four of us moved into middle age side-by-side, carving out our unique but intertwined paths toward death.

As we grew older, Richard remained perpetually unemployed, spending most of his time preoccupied with health problems and his own personal philosophical dilemmas. In the successes of others he saw evidence of the unfairness of the universe and thus a target against which to direct criticism. It wasn't that he was jealous of Kendrick, Colleen or I; it was more like he was frustrated with himself and by his own inability to be satisfied and happy with his life and the world he had built around himself. Nothing was ever quite right for Richard, and he came to spend a good deal of his time dissecting and diagnosing the reasons why this was the case.

Kendrick had always exhibited more of an aggressive, go-get-'em mentality than did Richard, but as he aged he developed from a free-spirited punk into a man consumed by the need for recognition and social status. Though, unlike Richard, he was regularly employed in good paying jobs, he constantly had problems dealing with his coworkers and his wife(s). Kendrick's driving desire was to be held in high esteem. He wanted to be an authority; a wise sage who others respected and would come to when they needed council and advice. His greatest frustration was that no one – not his coworkers nor his friends nor his wife(s) – thought of him in this way. Perhaps as a result of this, a sense of suspicion lay behind Kendrick's interactions with others, as if everyone he encountered was keeping some sort of vicious secret from him.

Colleen, my fire-haired punk-rock girl, like everyone else, descended into a mid-life crisis as she got older, trying to figure out who she was and how she fit into the world while passing into her 40's. She became preoccupied with the troubling realization that she was steadily aging, and instead of bringing wisdom, her age was instead bringing an increasingly profound fear of death. Every detail of her life was a reflection of this fear, including her dreams, her fascination with existentialist philosophy and her commitment to vigorous exercise.

Colleen and I were married, and like her I became increasingly terrified of my mortality and preoccupied with meditating on the seeming absurdity of life. In this way Colleen and I were either a good match or a horrible match, depending on your perspective.

In our friends, Richard and Kendrick, we found distraction from our personal worries at the same time that we gained insight into our own situations. But I suppose that's the way it is with all friends. In dealing with them, your attention is, on one level, drawn away from yourself. However, the sorts of friends that stay with you and that you find yourself spending time with over the years also serve a sort of therapeutic purpose. They reflect your needs and concerns in a way that words never can. They become a part of your universe, and thus become a part of who you are. They encircle you the way that planets constellate around one another, creating orbiting systems. You see yourself in your friends, they see themselves in you, and though sometimes it is aggravating, the tension thus created draws you close, like the gravity between the Earth and the Moon.

II.

Ultimately we were all the same. We all formed a unit. It was only the superficial differences between us, like our daily habits and the food we liked to eat that served to shield us from this deep truth. It was easy to point to these sorts of differences in order to reinforce our uniqueness. I liked berry pie, but Colleen hated it. Kendrick hated horror movies but I loved them. Richard loved mathematics, but I didn't. We all had our peculiar tastes, but everything that frustrated me about Richard, Kendrick and Colleen, just as everything I loved about them, really was a part of me as well.

III.

The deepest and most profound bond we all shared was the truth of our mortality. We were all destined to grow old, suffer and to die. This bond connected us not only to one another, but also to my colleagues at school, my mother and to every other human being in the world.

IV.

I guess the fact that as teenagers we all felt drawn to punk rock says something about a preexisting point of contact between our psychologies. We already thought of ourselves as misfits and outsiders, and we were eager to find other misfits and outsiders with whom we could share our feelings of alienation.

V.

I remember as a teenager, walking in the City with Kendrick. We were on our way to see a band perform, and as we walked to the club, Kendrick behaved in the exaggerated and rebellious way that punk rock teenagers often tended to behave. He was yelling and spitting at passing cars, insulting everyone on the street for being conventional members of the "system."

I was laughing, encouraging his obnoxiousness. He was right, after all. We were different from all of the stupid people around us who drove fancy cars, held down respectable jobs and who played the roles of respectable citizens.

"What a bunch of drones," Kendrick said, half disgusted and half amused. That he needed to vocalize this particular sentiment to me was symptomatic of the fact that he wanted to see and hear that I supported his assertion. He needed evidence that I agreed with him and that I was there to stand behind him in defiance of "them." In lashing out against "them" he was seeking to form a bond with me.

"Yeah, fuck 'em all," I laughed. I sincerely felt filled with contempt at the time; there was nothing fake in my utterance. I hated all of these people around me, even though I knew none of them. Thus, there was nothing personal about the sentiment; it was just an ontological expression of what I was at that moment. I felt intense hostility toward the undifferentiated mass of everyone "out there" who was not a part of my world. The individuals who passed by us on foot or in their cars were symbols of otherness to me, not flesh and blood people. To me they represented everything that I was against and everything I was fighting to avoid becoming. My only ally at that moment was Kendrick. We were like fellow soldiers battling against an army of drones.

I recall that one of these "drones" took offense at our behavior that night. He was driving down the street in a slick and expensive looking sports car. Sitting next to him in the passenger seat was a blonde woman, all made up and dressed to go out on the town. Everything in their appearance made me hate them. They were well-to-do, attractive and seemed not to be worried about anything except having a good time. Nothing in their behavior hinted at a fear of death or of anxiety or of a lack of self-confidence. They seemed to have no clue as to how screwed up the world was, how unhappy I was, or how pissed off Kendrick was.

As the car slowly passed by us in stop and go traffic, Kendrick spat in the passenger's face and kicked the side of the vehicle. "Fuck you, yuppie," he barked.

The sports car came to an abrupt halt and the male driver bounded out, appearing before us on the sidewalk. His girlfriend or wife or whoever the blonde passenger was angrily yelled for her partner to kick our asses.

As this unfolded I remember wondering, first of all, how old these two people were. At that time I perceived everyone who was not a part of my punk rock world as an elder, and such was my quick conclusion in this circumstance. Because I thought of this approaching man as someone older than me, I felt indignant that he was acting in such an aggressive manner. My gut reaction was that, as an adult, he should turn the other cheek, take the high ground and behave in a mature manner. Instead, here he was bringing himself down to a teenager's level. In my mind this fully justified what came next.

As the driver approached us, Kendrick spat in his face and yelled, "Fuck you!"

I yelled at the guy to just get back in his car.

The guy took a swing at Kendrick, striking him in the side of the head. Apparently the punch was not very powerful, since Kendrick did not fall, but stood his ground and continued to taunt Mr. Sports Car, calling him a "Yuppie Prick."

It was then, completely unannounced and unexpected by everyone present, that a figure appeared like a blur. At first I didn't recognize who it was, but when the figure tackled the yuppie and knocked him to the ground, I felt exhilarated. As it turned out, this blurred figure was an acquaintance of ours by the name of Derek. He had also been on his way to the show, saw what was happening, and, like a comrade in arms, intervened to offer us assistance. As he lay on top of the now very frightened yuppie, Kendrick and I swooped in and began to kick our victim anywhere that we could find an opening. I planted a few solid kicks in his ribs and I saw the toe of Kendrick's boot strike the yuppie's head at least once. I must report, though it now sounds atrocious, it was a wonderful feeling to pummel this man. This was, after all, not a real human being that we were assaulting, but a symbol of everything that we hated. We were paying the world back for all of the indignities and all of the humiliation that we felt we had suffered so far during our teenage lives. Each time our boots struck this man's body, I felt an increasing sense of power. I felt as if my greatest enemies were nothing and that so long as I stood with my friends, no one could hurt us.

The blonde in the car never left the vehicle, but I do remember the glee I felt when the angry tone in her voice was replaced by one of fear and panic. I don't recall her exact words, but I do remember the spirit of what she yelled to her companion: Get back in the car! Wasn't that what I told him to do in the first place? The change in her attitude was something I wanted to savor, and as the man we had just attacked finally made his way back to the vehicle, I did savor that moment. We had won. Fuck him and his girlfriend.

Fuck everyone.

VI.

Hatred is something that we normally think of as an emotion that is felt by us. At times, however, it becomes not just something that you feel, but a part of what you are. At those times, you don't feel hatred; hatred is felt through you.

VII.

It was quite common, when we were teenagers, for street preachers to be attracted to the large groups of strangely dressed kids who would congregate at the entrances of punk rock venues. In us they saw a chance to save souls and make a difference in the lives of the youth. I recall standing outside of a nightclub with Richard one evening when a middle-aged man, carrying an armful of pamphlets, approached us.

"Have you ever thought about where your life is going?" he asked us.

"That's a very vague question," Richard responded. "Exactly what do you mean by 'where my life is going'?"

"I mean," the man responded, "have you ever considered that the way you are now living your life is sinful and that it will end up killing you?"

I felt myself filling with rage at the insinuations of this preacher, and I could likewise see that Richard was fuming. Richard's anger, however, was more focused on the linguistic vagueness of the man's utterances than it was on his thinly veiled accusations against our morality.

"You keep talking about 'my life' as if you know exactly who I am and what I do. Until you clarify and specify exactly what it is that you mean, your questions are complete nonsense!" Richard exclaimed.

It made me feel good to see Richard get angry with this preacher and to articulate his objections. Normally, Richard was shy and unsure of himself. He usually acted awkward and hesitant. However, when confronted with someone like this street preacher, Richard really came into his own. He was quite confident and self-assured when it came to recognizing the gaps and flaws in the arguments of other people. Seeing Richard react in this way made me feel more assured that our opponent was, in fact, being unreasonable. Richard's assertive critique of the preacher's questions was like an alarm going off, signaling to me that I was correct to be annoyed.

"Your life is a life of sin!" the preacher responded. "You and your friends come out here dressed up in your punk rock clothes, doing drugs, drinking, fornicating and thinking that life is all fun and games!

But this will lead you to Hell. In the end, you will be sorry unless you accept Jesus Christ as your personal savior."

"How do you know that I do drugs, drink and fornicate? Can you tell that from my 'punk rock clothes'?" Richard spat back. There was a laugh in his voice, mixed in with the anger, suggesting to both the preacher and me that there was very little to take seriously here.

"So are you saying that you don't do those things? Can you honestly tell me that you are living your life according to Christian values?"

Richard's shoulders convulsed as he started laughing. "I wish I had someone to fornicate with! The only reason why I don't do those things is because I don't have the resources! If only I had some money and a girlfriend I would be having all the sex and doing all of the drugs and drinking all of the booze I possibly could!"

"So you admit that you are not a Christian?" The preacher now saw his opportunity.

"I don't know," Richard said. "How exactly do you define a Christian?"

At this the preacher held out his stack of pamphlets. "It's all here in black and white. If you want to know how it is that Jesus wants us to live our lives, all you need to do is read this. All of the answers are here."

I shot a quick glance at Richard, and he shot one back at me. Nonchalantly, I reached into my jacket pocket for my lighter. We were standing so close to the street preacher and his outstretched pile of literature that I was able unobtrusively to hold the flame of the lighter beneath his stack of papers. As he was so focused on Richard, the preacher did not immediately notice that his pamphlets had ignited.

"It says in Revelations that the flames of Hell will be the fitting punishment for those who reject God! You will suffer eternal torment and pain because of your sinful ways! The righteous will watch from Heaven and witness how the will of God is done! Do you want to burn and suffer forever? If not, you must accept Jesus now, before it is too late!"

Many of the people standing outside of the club noticed what was going on, and a few of them had gathered around, laughing at the ironical scene unfolding before them.

"Hey buddy," one of the bystanders shouted out, "I think God is sending *you* a message!"

It was then the preacher finally noticed that his pamphlets were being consumed in fire. Instinctively, he dropped the whole stack of materials onto the sidewalk, causing them to spread out on the ground and to flare up in a renewed and more violent blaze. Sparks flew up into the air as the papers hit the pavement, and the assembled crowd let out a collective vocalization.

"Whoooahhhhhh!!!!"

The preacher, on the other hand, just stood there, hands at his side, appearing quite defeated. He shook his head slowly back and forth, never looking any of us in the eye. The expression on his face was the expression of a person who felt impotent and unsure of what to do next, although I also think I detected a slight look of pity. Whether this was a look directed toward us or toward himself, I could not determine.

The only words out of the preacher's mouth were, "You will all burn in Hell." He kept repeating this sentence, over and over as he shook his head and stared at the heap of ashes at his feet.

"We all suffer and die. That's it. No Hell, no Heaven; nothing." I taunted.

The preacher didn't say anything. He just walked away as everyone in front of the club continued laughing.

VIII.

We graduated from being spectators at shows to forming our own band called Nihilism. I was the singer, Colleen played the guitar, Kendrick played drums and Richard was on bass. Our music was simple, fast and aggressive. The lyrics of the songs dealt with a variety of themes – political, moral, philosophical – but whatever the subject, the tone was always cynical and angry. We played shows whenever and wherever the opportunity arose.

Nihilism had a small but enthusiastic following in our hometown. Our shows never failed to attract a crowd of punks who would slam dance and sing along with the songs, creating an atmosphere in which the boundaries between band and audience seemed to melt away. We all became one inside the club, sharing the common experience of being there together and allowing the same emotions to wash over us. As one we were all angry. As one, we were all jubilant. As one, we were all melancholy. People I otherwise did not know became my brothers and sisters simply through the visceral power of music, and this state of enchantment could be induced again and again, recurrently, on differing evenings simply by playing the same songs.

One night we played a show in the most unlikely of places: a functioning glass warehouse. The warehouse was rented out to a local promoter for a small fee with the understanding that all of the merchandise would remain safely protected behind wood panels lining the walls of the space. The cost of any broken goods would come out of promoter's own pocket. When we first walked into the place, the only hint that there were large quantities of breakable materials stored here was the tell-tale glint of the edges of glass sheets that peeked out, about 20 feet above the floor, from their plywood enclosures. Only about a foot of the glass was visible behind the protective barriers, but I imagined that the sheets had to be long enough to reach halfway to the floor.

There were four bands on the bill that evening. We went on second, just before a band called Ruins of Society, who in turn preceded the main act, which was a very well known band called Teeth! All of the opening bands played tremendously that night, but when it came to the famous headliners, things fell apart. The lead singer was so intoxicated that he had problems standing up. As he mounted the stage, he fell down and lay moaning into the microphone in an incomprehensible and pathetic manner. Throughout the band's set, he repeatedly tried to get to his feet, but repeatedly ended up collapsing. Later, I learned that he was on heroin. Though at the time we laughed at and taunted the helpless singer, in retrospect it was really a sad and depressing situation: the vital and liberating energy of punk undermined by slavish addiction to a stupid drug.

After the show, while the assembled crowd remained to socialize, drink and horse around, Jason, the bass player from Ruins of Society and I approached the promoter to collect our money. We had been promised a measly $50 for our performances; enough to pay for gas and beer.

"Sorry dudes, but I barely have enough to cover what I promised *Teeth!*," the guy told us, emphasizing the name "*Teeth!*" as if it held some kind of self-evident power that would make us back off from our request.

"Did you even see how fucked up that singer was?!" I responded, harboring the misguided thought that somehow payment should be commensurate with the quality of a band's performance. "He couldn't even stand up!"

"Sorry, man. I promised them."

"I don't give one fuck what you promised *them*," Jason yelled, looking like an angry Aryan in a leather jacket, "You promised *us* 50 bucks!"

The promoter now looked scared. He didn't say a word, but just stood there looking at Jason, slack-jawed and silent. I wouldn't have been surprised if his knees had start knocking together.

"You piece of shit!" Jason screamed, leaning in to get face to face with the promoter, who still didn't move or say a thing. As if he didn't know what else to do, Jason cleared his throat in a slow, exaggerated show, filled his mouth with phlegm and then spat the wad into the promoter's face, right between the eyes. The wad of phlegm stuck for an instant, and then slowly dripped down his nose and over his lips. He never even made a move to wipe it off.

Jason stomped away, but I stayed in place just long enough to give Mr. Promoter an up and down look before saying, "You've got some spit on your face."

When I told the rest of our band that we had been stiffed for our $50, they were pissed off. Kendrick in particular fumed, yelling about how he wanted to kick ass. But Richard silenced him with a simple, elegant suggestion.

"We can still make him pay," he said, looking up at the glinting edges of glass panes that peaked up seductively from behind their plywood enclosures.

Colleen, Kendrick and I all looked at one another and started laughing. We had been sharing 40 ounce bottles of malt liquor between us, and now we all realized that these bottles offered a fitting solution to our present dilemma. Kendrick was the first to down the remaining contents of his bottle in a few gulps before hoisting it behind his head like a large grenade and then stopping to gauge the trajectory required to deliver the ordinance to it's destination. There was only a small area of unprotected glass high above our heads, but with a masterful heave, Kendrick arced his bottled into the air and through the opening behind which the glass pane was protected.

The noise level inside of the warehouse was high. The crowds of people who were talking, in addition to the recorded music that was now playing, made it impossible to hear the smashing sounds of glass. When Kendrick's projectile found its target, however, we could see the top edge of one of the sheets disappear, collapsing behind its enclosure like a waterfall of crystal shards. Colleen let out a "Whooop!" and was the next to down her beer and then launch her bottle upwards. It also made contact, bringing yet another sheet of glass crashing down.

Once out of our own bottles, we scavenged empties from around the warehouse, and, one by one, we heaved them into the openings along the walls. One by one, the tops of the glass panes disappeared from view until we finally felt as if we had been adequately compensated for our services that night.

IX.

The Russian anarchist Bakunin wrote that destruction is a creative act. This is true. It clears the ground, making room for new things.

But destruction is also an expressive act.

It is also a spiteful act.

It is also sometimes a necessary act.

Destruction is inevitable in a world where nothing is permanent.

X.

People change over time; but they also stay the same.

We are thrown into a world not of our own making, and as we grow older we fight to express ourselves through actions and words that are never quite perfect, but which nevertheless come to define who we become. We do the things we do because the world is out of joint with some ideal image we have of the way things should be. In this, every single one of our concrete actions falls short of its goal. Yet, if we scrutinize the patterns and the rhythms involved in the unfolding of our actions, a truth emerges from their totality the way that the plot of a novel emerges out of the collected letters, words, paragraphs and chapters that it contains.

CHAPTER EIGHT: THE DIAGNOSIS

I.

N ow this may be a bit uncomfortable, but just hold on. It'll be over in a few minutes."

The nurse sounded reassuring, but the aching pain that radiated from my intestines was not. I was lying on an X-ray table with a tube inserted in my rectum while a liquid mixture was being forced into my colon. I felt like I was at the point of bursting, but the nurse kept the flow constant.

"Just a little bit more."

"I don't think that I can hold this in much longer," I confided.

I really was getting worried since I didn't want to shit all over the examination room. With the amount of pressure that had built up inside me, I figured the contents of my intestines could very well end up painting the entire wall behind me in filth.

"You're doing just fine," she reassured. But she wasn't the one with the hose up her butt.

After my bout of vomiting at the tenure dinner, I made an appointment to be seen by a doctor. The preliminary examination suggested that my problem might be an ulcer, so in order to investigate this hypothesis X-rays were ordered. The X-ray procedure involved flooding my lower GI tract with a barium enema (or as the nurse described it, a "pink milkshake") so that any abnormalities would be highlighted on the film. The process was described to me as "quick and involving mild discomfort," but that was the description of someone who obviously had never undergone the ordeal.

The tube was removed from my rear end and I was instructed to lie on my back. It was then that I saw the X-ray technician for the first time. He was standing above me, manipulating an intimidating looking piece of equipment into place above my midsection. The pain in the lower half of my body was so generalized that I needed to focus my attention on something, so I stared at the mechanical arm that held the machine fixed to the ceiling. Sweat was pouring off of my forehead and as I cinched up my rectal muscles, fighting off the natural desire to let go, the sweat spread to the rest of my body. I was swimming in perspiration and I feared that I would soon be swimming in my own excrement.

"Let's just snap a couple more pictures," the technician said. He wasn't really talking to me. It seemed like he was talking to himself. I might just as well have been a large, overfilled water balloon.

II.

When the X-rays were done, the nurse helped me off of the table and led me to the bathroom. With each step I felt as though I would explode. I imagined that if I tripped and fell on the floor I would certainly burst open like a watermelon dropped onto the sidewalk. The nurse closed the bathroom door behind me and I immediately rushed over to the toilet.

I guess I got confused. Something in my mind was telling me that since the enema had been liquid, it should exit through my urethra. I stood facing the toilet, prepared to urinate when a wave of intestinal peristalsis overcame me and I instantly realized that the "milkshake" was going to exit from the same place that it had entered. I spun around and luckily landed on the toilet in time for the contents of my bowels to empty into the appropriate receptacle. I stopped sweating and just sat with my head bowed. I had something to be thankful for at that very moment and nothing else mattered.

III.

Though will power has its limits, if a person desires to avoid certain consequences or to attain certain rewards with enough intensity, he or she can overcome even the most urgent natural impulses; at least temporarily.

IV.

An ulcer was not my problem. What I suffered from was a hiatal hernia. Part of my stomach had popped up over my diaphragm producing all of my discomfort and symptoms. The condition was chronic, but probably was aggravated by the stress I had been experiencing while working toward tenure. It probably was the cause of the sudden onset of pain and vomiting at the tenure dinner. Apparently the condition is really not that unusual. The doctor told me that more than 40% of the population suffers from just this malady and that surgery or special treatment is not necessary. He suggested a variety of practical, common sense steps to minimize the symptoms:

1. Don't eat too soon before bed.

2. Raise the head of your bed. This way stomach acid will stay put and not flow up into your esophagus.

3. Avoid caffeine and smoking.

4. Avoid acidy foods.

5. Use antacids when necessary.

V.

Richard came to visit me at home one day after my diagnosis.
"How are you feeling?" He asked as I greeted him at the door.
"Well, I'm feeling a lot better than I did a few days ago."

Richard was a very tall man, but he was a very awkward tall
man. He commonly acted ill at ease and he always stooped slightly, as
if in an attempt to reduce his height to avoid being noticed. When he
walked it was like watching some sort of nervous cat. He loped along,
hunched and as low to the ground as he could get, aiming himself at
some resting place like a chair or the corner of the room where he could
blend in with the surroundings. Today that resting place was the couch
in my living room.

Richard wanted certainty in life. Over the years, this desire had
ironically led him into the situation that he rarely accomplished the
things that he wanted to do. Whenever he approached a task, he spent
all of his time trying to figure out the best method by which to attack
the project instead of actually engaging himself in its completion. He
would get bogged down in details while he reflected on plans, becoming
overly concerned with possible problems, finally deciding that the
project was not worthwhile because of all of the things that could
go wrong. It was frustrating to watch this occur over and over again.
School, jobs and relationships chronically slipped from his fingers as he
engaged in a destructive over-analysis of each situation.

What was ironic about Richard's attitude was that his tendency
toward analysis was borne of a desire for certainty yet ended up
delivering a thoroughly incomplete and uncertain life into his lap. He
enjoyed conceptually analyzing things, however, because, he claimed, it
gave him a feeling of control.

"It's like when you take your car apart and then put it back
together. You learn about each piece of the machine and how it all fits
together. It gives you a real feeling of satisfaction and a confidence that
you really know how it all works."

I didn't completely disagree, but I felt that I had to add the cautionary note, "Yeah. But you'd better be sure that you're able to put the whole thing back together or else you'll be left with a pile of junk."

VI.

Richard was brilliant, but he had never finished his Ph.D. The one sticking point for him was writing the dissertation. Each time that he tried to start writing, something struck him as wrong. There always seemed to be a missing or defective piece. Instead of working through the difficulty, he would stop, throw the whole thing away and start from scratch.

Richard said, "It doesn't make any sense to me to try and build a solid argument from bad parts. I'd rather just rethink the whole thing than end up with a patchwork of lies. The reason I began studying philosophy in the first place was in order to find some sort of truth that would act as a foundation for all of my future decisions."

Then I spoke. "But isn't there a point where one has to simply act upon the information that one has in order to progress anywhere? It seems to me that you reach a point where you have to stop questioning and analyzing everything as a matter of practicality. For instance, I could lie in bed thinking about the most efficient way to get up and go to the kitchen in the morning, but if I don't just get up at some point, even if it's not in accordance with the most optimal plan, I will never get breakfast and I'll never get to work."

Richard looked at me seriously. "That's a good example and I see your point. My concern is that people often times use practical concerns as an excuse for not thinking carefully. The philosopher is a person who devotes his life to the discovery of consistencies and inconsistencies. He thinks long and hard about issues usually regarded as matters of common sense to the vast majority of humanity, ferreting out and rectifying contradictions that have gone unnoticed or that have been ignored by everyone else. Most times his accomplishments are viewed as nothing more than impractical, academic exercises. But regardless of public opinion, the philosopher fulfills an important role in that his careful, analytic approach to everyday issues is aimed at the discovery of certainty and truth. The philosopher may himself be impractical, but his conclusions serve the rest of mankind. He thinks so that others may act.

VII.

Richard's ultimate concern was with achieving a state of psychological, rather than physical, comfort. He was willing to face a life of poverty and lack of accomplishment in financial and career matters so long as he was able to find psychological comfort in some sort of philosophic certainty. In essence, he wanted to achieve a mental state in which he no longer simply desired but rather possessed the truth. He desired to no longer desire, yet because his brand of psychological comfort could be achieved only in those situations where he recognized and resolved a previously unresolved dilemma, Richard was doomed to unending struggle. All resolutions lead to even further dilemmas, and therefore toward further psychological discomfort. Desiring not to desire was the engine powering the vehicle of Richard's philosophy, propelling him toward further philosophizing.

If Richard was taken as the model of the proper way to pursue philosophy, then philosophy was struggle, but it was the kind of struggle aimed at the end of struggle. Its ultimate goal was self-annihilation and eternal stasis. If it was possible that the world's final inconsistency could be resolved, the legacy of philosophy would be complete and historians would take over. Its final goal realized, its efficient cause exhausted, the philosophic struggle would end in a nihilistic terminus.

VIII.

The idealist vainly struggles to achieve the unattainable. Since the ideal is distinct from the real, the ideal must always remain other than real.

IX.

There were times when I didn't know what to say to Richard. Sometimes he would just stare at me as though he expected me to say something profound. When I finally did speak, he would act disappointed, as though what I had to say was nowhere near as important as he had been hoping. At such times he would get nit picky and insulting, pointing out the errors and inconsistencies in my logic. This was when I felt the poisoning effect of Richard's influence. His desire for clarity and certainty made me question myself and my own capability to penetrate the veil of life's mysteries.

At other times Richard preferred to insult and criticize himself. During these cycles he would stop in mid-sentence during conversation and refuse to continue talking because he thought he "wasn't making any sense." He hated informal theorizing, and when he found himself speculating on things that were unverifiable, he would call himself "stupid" and shift his attention to other things.

"It just doesn't make sense to talk about things that no one will ever be able to test according to a scientific method," he sometimes said. "It's like claiming that God exists. No one can ever prove or disprove such a claim. There is no consequence that follows from such an assertion, so why even make the assertion in the first place?"

"Well," I replied, "there are very few things that we know for certain. If we restricted our conversation and speculations only to those claims that could be positively proved or disproved, life would be pretty dull. Likewise, if we limited our actions to those that had certain outcomes, we wouldn't do too much. The people that I respect, in fact, are those who are adventurous enough to speak and act in circumstances of uncertainty. Though I understand the role of the timid, I admire the bold for their aggressive pursuit of the ambiguous."

I continued. "For instance, Oppenheimer became far more

interesting after he completed the atom bomb than he had been before hand. When he was forced to struggle with the moral uncertainty of his creation, he attained a real, tragic depth. There is something heroic about a person who brings value and meaning to circumstances that others see only in quantitative, technical terms."

Richard was shaking his head and rolling his eyes toward the roof.

"I don't understand what you're talking about," he sighed.

X.

Despite following the advice of my doctors, the pain in my stomach persisted, and in fact it got progressively worse as time went on. Each morning I would wake up with a dull, generalized ache radiating through my abdomen and chest. I could deal with the pain during the day when I was engaged in routine activities, but at night when I tried to get to sleep, it was impossible to think of anything except the discomfort. I began to worry more and more that the doctor's expert opinion on my condition was wrong.

Perhaps he was just misinterpreting my symptoms.

CHAPTER NINE: NIGHTMARES

I.

A re you going to eat chalk for the rest of your life?"
Kendrick had taken to asking me this same question
every time that I unwrapped an antacid tablet and popped it into my
mouth.

"The doctor told me that whenever I feel any discomfort I
should just eat an antacid tablet. It's Doctor's orders," I smiled.

Kendrick looked disgusted and shook his head.

"Do you expect to go through the rest of your life taking that
stuff?"

I shrugged.

Kendrick just kept shaking his head and giving me that look.
It was the look given to the utterly pathetic. I had seen him give it to
panhandling drunks on the street, yuppies, cripples, and the mentally
retarded. It was the "I feel sorry for you" look that makes the recipient
feel less than fully human. I hated being looked at that way.

"Would you lighten up!?" I moaned.

"Well, I bet if you took better care of yourself you could
alleviate the symptoms. You worry too much. You need to stop worrying
so much."

"Worrying has nothing to do with it. I have something

physically wrong."

Kendrick just shook his head and continued to look at me with that annoying expression.

II.

The painful burning in my chest and abdomen did not seem to be getting any better, but that was just what the doctor said would be the case. I was in the position of simply managing the symptoms unless I decided to opt for major surgery. I preferred taking antacid tablets to going under the knife.

My sleeping habits were severely disrupted. It was inevitable that the burning feeling in my chest would become very intense when I lay down, and it would become even worse if I tried to lie on my stomach. The effects of the antacid tablets usually wore off just as I drifted into sleep, and I either woke up or experienced bizarre nightmares. The nightmares I didn't mind so much. At least they were interesting.

III.

I was sitting in the cafe when the stranger approached me. I can't remember what his face looked like. He walked up to the table where I was seated and delivered his message: "Colleen's dead."

I was shocked by the message and annoyed by his deadpan delivery.

As he walked out of the coffee house, panic shot through my body. It ping-ponged around in my skull for a micro-second and then rocketed down my throat, through my esophagus and out my anus. By the time that the panic had exited my body I was left with an acidy, parched and jittery feeling that I had come to be acquainted with numerous times in the past after drinking too much coffee. The reaction that I experienced was enough to divert my thoughts from the message I had just received. I looked at my hands. They were shaking.

I stood up to leave when the stranger's words echoed in my head: "Colleen's dead."

Once again the sensation of panic shot through my body. The feeling that I associated with over indulgence in coffee lingered afterwards. I stumbled to a pay phone and a quarter appeared in my hand. I dropped it into the coin slot and dialed a number.

"County Hospital," came the voice from the other end of the line.

"Is Colleen there?" I stammered.

"No. She's dead."

A long, electric pulse of panic passed through the center of my body. It was about a foot in diameter and a yard long. It pushed its way through my digestive tract and seared all of the flesh in its path. The incredible heat radiated by the shaft of panic boiled away all of the liquids in my body and I was reduced to a heap of ash.

IV.

Initially, I couldn't move when I woke up from that nightmare. I was lying on my back staring at the ceiling.

Beside me lay Colleen. Her face peeked out from underneath the blankets. It was only when I noticed her relaxed breathing that I was able to move my own body. I poked Colleen in the shoulder to wake her up, or more precisely, in order to confirm that she was alive. She groaned and opened up her eyes. She was annoyed and scowling.

"What?" she angrily mumbled.

"I dreamt that you were dead," I explained.

She was already asleep again by the time that I spoke.

I got out of bed and looked at the clock. It was 7 AM. I scratched my head as I walked to the bathroom. The tile floor was very cold and shocked me into a state of wakefulness. I sat down on the toilet. It was just as cold as the floor. The only thing that wasn't cold was my digestive tract. It burned with stomach acid, so I reached for the jar of antacid sitting on the bathroom counter.

V.

There are a variety of theories about the meaning and function of dreams. Freud claimed that dreams result from the lowering of inhibitions during sleep. That is when our wishes and anxieties, unhindered by social conditioning and norms, come to the fore. The "id" instincts can then express themselves, cloaked in the symbolism of dream images, providing a relief valve for repressed desires and urges.

Recent theories, on the other hand, emphasize the meaninglessness of dreams. According to these theories, dreams are simply the garbage of the mind. Every night, that garbage must be dumped so that our rational minds don't get too cluttered with information; like dumping the cache on your computer so that your web browser will function properly.

My dreams, I've decided, come from my body. The pain in my stomach produces the images in my mind. In one sense they are meaningful. They represent a cry for help from my gut. In another sense they are meaningless. They are simply an epiphenomenon of my malady.

My philosophy has much in common with my dreams.

VI.

"I've come to the conclusion that there are only two reasons to read fiction," I grumbled.

Kendrick was scrutinizing me with his disapproving look. He knew that I was grumpy, and he knew that at times like these I acted the way that he acted normally; like a cynical jerk.

"What are those reasons?" he asked.

"Well first, if the fiction is especially well written. Someone who is really good with putting words together deserves to be read. Reading a well-written piece of fiction is kind of like looking at a well-done painting. You may not like the subject matter, but you can appreciate the talent and skill of the artist."

"The second reason is if the author has an especially important point to make. In that case the fictional work is just a vehicle to get an interesting or important point across, and you can appreciate the subject matter even if the author lacks artistic talent or skill."

"All other fiction is useless. I mean, if a person can't write well or doesn't have an important point to make, why read the story? Anyone can make up a story. When I was a kid I used to read lots of horror novels. I loved them. Then one day I was reading this book about people who were turned into zombies by some sort of mad scientist, and half way through I thought to myself, 'Why am I reading this? I could just make up my own story.' I put the book down and never picked up another novel until after college."

Kendrick looked annoyed.

"There are plenty of other reasons to read fiction," he responded. "Sometimes I just want to escape. A good horror, science fiction or fantasy novel is an effective tool for that purpose. Sometimes I want to be thrilled. A good adventure novel is what I read in those cases. Sometimes I want to laugh, so I read a piece of humor. There are as many reasons to read fiction as there are genres of fiction. I think your two reasons are rather limiting."

"Bah!" I spat, and reached for another antacid tablet. "You must have very little imagination if you need someone else to make up stories to thrill or humor you. I can make things up for myself. Either that or I take a nap and enjoy my own dreams."

VIII.

One of my recurring dreams didn't even have a story line that it followed. In this dream I was traveling around an oval course in space. It wasn't my body that was moving, but my awareness. I went round and round, slowly cycling along the path.

At one end of the oval, I experienced a feeling of well-being and comfort. When I was at that end of the path, there was a pleasant hum that filled the air and I felt a warm, soft sensation all around me.

However, as I moved away from that end of the oval path and toward the opposite end, the sensations that I experienced began to be unpleasant. The hum in the air became a shrill, loud screech and the warm soft feeling became burning discomfort.

As the dream went on, I simply vacillated between these two poles. As I moved around the oval path, I knew what to expect. When I was at the comfortable end of the path, I dreaded my journey toward the other end, and when I was at the uncomfortable end, I looked forward to being back where it was pleasant. I just moved back and forth over the course of my dream, like a marble caught in a circular track.

IX.

Colleen also suffered from recurrent nightmares. I was often awakened at some point in the middle of the night by her vocalizations and movements. Sometimes she screamed, sometimes she yelled obscenities, and sometimes she lashed out, kicking or hitting me.

Her nightmares always had the same underlying theme. A dark, male figure was stalking her and she was trying to get away. She was always frustrated in her efforts to flee, however. She would trip and fall, or try to hide in a too obvious spot and the stalker would catch up to her. It was at that point that she would start screaming in her dream and in real life.

Colleen claimed that in her dreams, she knew that if she yelled and moved around that she would be able to wake herself up. She was aware at some level that she was dreaming, but this awareness did nothing to alleviate the fear that was conjured up during the course of the dream episode.

"What do you think causes your nightmares?" I asked her once.

"I don't know," she answered. "Sometimes I think they have

something to do with my feeling that life is out of control. In the dreams I feel like I'm completely powerless to stave off the man who is following me. I've noticed that it is the same feeling I get at the times when I'm most frustrated at work, or with you or with members of my family."

"At other times I think my dreams are just nonsense," she added.

"You know, in German a nightmare is called an *Alptraum*. It literally means a 'dream about the alps.' I wonder how they came up with that."

Colleen nodded. "It makes sense if you think about it. Mountain climbers experience many of the same feelings of powerlessness that I experience in my nightmares. As they push their bodies to the brink of their capabilities, they become aware of how insignificant they are. They could die on the slopes of the mountain, but the mountain wouldn't care. Whether a climber makes it to the top is of no consequence to the mountain. The climber is nothing to it; and that awareness is frightening."

"The very thing that nightmares are made of. It makes me think of those mystics who torture themselves in order to achieve spiritual enlightenment. Sometimes the only way to really turn inward and confront yourself is to subdue the flesh."

X.

Pieces of fiction, dreams and philosophies are the complicated mental consequences of somatic stimulus. The first link in the causal chain leading to the writing of a piece of fiction, to a dream or to a philosophy is a source of discomfort that makes the author aware of himself or herself. The body is the first point of contact between the outside world of physical existence and the inside world of the mind, but the body is also capable of producing its own forms of internal discomfort independent of the outside world.

My body talks unambiguously to my mind through the burning in my gut, but my mind is like some sort of insane artist that interprets everything in wild and imaginative ways.

My body and mind just don't understand each other.

CHAPTER TEN: THE HEADQUARTERS

I.

When I first told my mother that I was going to move out of her house, she was resistant. "I don't see why you need to spend money on an apartment when you can live with me rent free," she said. "After all, it will be lonely here without you."

"I just need to establish some independence," I told her. The truth was that I felt rather sheltered. Moving in with friends and living in the City would be a step in the direction of learning how to navigate the world on my own. It wasn't that I looked forward to moving out; it just felt like something I *should* do.

And so, when I was 20, I moved into a run down, two bedroom flat with Colleen, Kendrick and Richard. Colleen and I shared a room, Richard occupied the other bedroom while Kendrick used the main living room for his space. We referred to our new digs as "The Headquarters."

My mother never visited.

II.

Our place was more like a clubhouse than a home. There were few rules, and a steady stream of guests and visitors made the place feel like an ongoing party was taking place. This was where people would rendezvous before heading off to see a band or to hang out at a bar. After the shows were over, or after the bars closed, this was where people ended up, sleeping on the floors or in the closets until they were ready to head back to their own homes.

The street on which our building sat was busy. It was away from the city center, but still bustling with activity: pedestrians flooded the sidewalks and cars flowed in a never ending river back and forth in front of our living room windows. Our apartment occupied the entire floor on the second storey of the building. Below was a smaller, one bedroom flat as well as a garage. Above was another two bedroom flat, identical in layout to our own. Our neighbors changed regularly over the course of the time we occupied our place, and we usually had problems getting along with them.

III.

I was sitting in the breakfast nook at the Headquarters one morning, drinking my coffee and mentally sorting through the things I had planned for the day when Kendrick walked into the kitchen, completely naked.

"What the fuck are you doing? Why don't you put some clothes on?!" I was annoyed at being subjected to Kendrick's bare flesh. His little penis was nestled into his pubic hair like some sort of tiny snake in a nest of black grass while the pimples scattered across his chest, back and ass shone against his pale skin like tiny rubies. There was something embarrassingly vulnerable as well as threateningly aggressive about his display. The contradiction was unbearable to me.

"What's the problem? Are you uncomfortable with nudity?" He laughed. We were learning new things about one another day by day.

"I don't want to look at your ugly body while I'm eating," I retorted, going back to my coffee.

Instead of retreating, Kendrick came even closer to where I was sitting, standing with his crotch poised right at my eye level. I could see every hair, mole and pimple. Not wanting to yield my ground, I tried to think of the best way to make him back off, deciding that the fear of pain was probably the best choice. My lighter – the one I had used to ignite the street preacher's papers – was in my pocket, and so I pulled it out, struck the flint and held it's flame threateningly close to his dick.

"I'll burn it off," I warned.

Kendrick laughed. "No you won't."

With that, I touched the flame to his pubic hair, which caught fire. A sheet of flame swept from his balls to his belly, leaving a singed dark patch and the horrible smell of burned hair. Kendrick grabbed his crotch and leapt backwards, his eyes wide with disbelief.

"You motherfucker!" he yelled, and ran out of the kitchen laughing.

I was laughing as well, thinking that everything was done, when Kendrick reappeared, still naked, but now accompanied by Richard and Derek, who were also naked. They crowded around me, pushing close and wagging their flaccid pricks to and fro.

"What's the matter? Can't you appreciate the natural human form?" Kendrick taunted, giggling and choking on his own words. He obviously thought this was all great fun.

"Get away from me!" I laughed, annoyed but also amused. I got up from the table and pushed past my three naked friends, cringing as I felt their soft, flabby flesh against my arms.

As I tried to get away, my pals followed me down the hallway and into the living room. The window was open, allowing in the sounds of the street while also offering the people outside a clear view of three naked punk rockers dancing and jumping about ridiculously. In defense, I once again pulled out my lighter, brandishing it in front of me, like a villager from a horror movie fending off monsters with a torch. We were all laughing, although I was feeling increasingly uncomfortable. I was ready for this game to be over.

Kendrick reached for a newspaper that was lying on the seat of an old, torn easy chair in the corner of the room. Still dancing around, he rolled the newspaper into a tube and, imitating me, began waving it around in front of himself as if it was some sort of weapon.

"You're not scaring me with that, you fuckin' nudist!" I warned.

Kendrick screwed up his face in an exaggerated expression of disappointment, and then said, "Well then, I may have to use poison!" He took the rolled up newspaper and put it behind his back. He bent forward and, sticking his ass out, started wiggling back and forth. Richard and Derek both jumped away from him when they saw what he was doing, exclaiming "Ohhhhhhhhhh!" simultaneously in disgust. He had stuck the end of the rolled up newspaper into his asshole.

"En Garde!" Kendrick yelled, now waving the shit covered newspaper like a sword. There was a brown stain on the end of the tube where it had penetrated his rectum. The smell of feces was quickly permeating the air.

"You're fuckin' sick!" I yelled, truly disgusted and recoiling from the contaminated paper. Now I really was vulnerable. Kendrick held all of the power here, as none of us was willing to come into contact with his shit stick. He had the ultimate weapon.

But I had fire. Fire beats paper.

As he continued to swing the rolled up, shit stained newspaper back and forth, I did the same with my lighter. Our duel went on for a minute or so before the newspaper burst into flames and Kendrick, not quite knowing what to do, tossed the flaming tube out of the front window. It arced across the living room and through the opening, falling out of view and into the street below. As one, we all dove to the ground, wanting to disappear from the view of those outside. None of us wanted to be held accountable for depositing a shit covered, flaming projectile onto the head of a passerby.

We crawled over to the window, and one by one poked our heads over the sill. Peering down on the street, we immediately saw where it was that the newspaper had landed. It lay, black and mostly disintegrated, on the hood of a car. It was my Cutlass Supreme, and Colleen was standing next to it.

"You fuckin' idiots!" She screamed, seeing us all peeking over the ledge of the window.

We all burst into a renewed round of laughter.

IV.

It's all fun and games until someone gets an eye put out.

V.

One evening after Nihilism played a show, we returned to the Headquarters with friends, a few hangers-on and a lot of beer. The front living room, Kendrick's space, was set up as the center of festivities, with people lying on the couch and on the floor. A handful of guys and girls gathered around the record player, spinning music. Kendrick had invited a couple of girls that none of us knew to come along, and he and Derek spent most of the night socializing and obviously trying to sleep with whoever proved to be receptive. As the break of dawn approached, most of the guests had left except for the two girls.

Richard left for work and Colleen and I went to bed. Our room shared a wall with the living room, so every time that there was a loud burst of laugher, or when the music gained in volume, we could hear the goings on. There was a lot of giggling emanating from behind the wall, and periodically we could here something like thumping noises that we chalked up to Kendrick or Derek stomping around, getting more beer, or returning from the bathroom.

I had drifted off to sleep when I suddenly was awakened by an especially loud commotion. There was still a lot of giggling, so I surmised that everything was OK. The giggling was accompanied by what sounded like the dragging of large items across the floor.

"Hee, hee, hee, tee hee!"

Scrape! Drag! Bump!

"Hee, hee, hee!"

Colleen woke up shortly after I did, looking annoyed. "What time is it?" she asked.

"It's 7am."

"What the fuck are they doing?"

"Those girls are still here. I'm not sure that I want to know what they're doing," I responded, only half in jest.

The two of us lay there, now wide awake, waiting for the next intrusive noise.

"Bump, bump, bump."

"Hee, hee, hee."

Suddenly there was the sound of someone jumping up and running out of the living room. The footsteps came fast and heavy, going down the hallway and out the front door. We could hear the sound of the garage opening, then closing, and then the sounds of the heavy footsteps coming back up the front stairs, down the hallway and back into the living room. More giggling.

"Hee, hee, hee."

I looked at Colleen and we both rolled our eyes.

After a pause, there was the sound of an explosion. Colleen and I jumped up and let out simultaneous yelps. I dove out of bed and toward the door of the bedroom. As I opened the door, a cloud of smoke billowed into our room, rushing like an upside down waterfall pouring onto the ceiling. Running into the hallway I could see that the entire living room was filled with smoke, and it was steadily spreading to the rest of the flat, undulating along the ceilings and entering the other rooms.

And then there was more giggling. "Hee, hee, hee."

I rushed into the living room to find Kendrick and Derek busily opening the windows and trying to clear out the accumulated smoke. Their girlfriends were lying on the floor, in front of the fireplace, giggling and laughing. The fireplace was the source of the smoke, I could see, and there was a prominent black mark emanating from the fire box and up onto the wall above it. On the floor next to one of the girls was a gasoline can.

Kendrick turned to look at me. He wore an expression that showed a mixture of amusement and apprehension. His eyebrows were raised in a surprised sort of way, his eyes were very wide, but his mouth was formed into a tight, small grin.

"We couldn't get the fire lit, so we thought we'd use a bit of gasoline to get things going," he explained.

"You're a fuckin' idiot," I spat out. "You could've killed us all!" I then silently turned and went back to my bed.

VI.

Sometimes your best friends can also be your worst enemies.

VII.

I found four hypodermic syringes scattered on the living room floor next to Kendrick and the two partially clothed girls. Derek had left the apartment by the time I arose from my unsettled sleep around noon, and it looked like Kendrick and his friends would be out of it for the rest of the day.

"I don't know how long I can take this," I told Colleen. "I love these guys, but I can't stand living like this. I wish we just had a house of our own that was quiet and tidy; a place where we didn't have to deal with this sort of nonsense."

Colleen and I left for a late breakfast, returning a few hours later in the afternoon.

VIII.

We arrived back at the Headquarters to find it surrounded by police cars. When we tried to enter the building, an officer stopped us on the stairs and told us that we could not go inside.

"But we live here. What's going on?" I said, already fearing something really bad. I suspected that someone was hurt. I was scared. I didn't know what I should do.

"You live here? Come this way," the officer said, taking me by the arm and motioning to Colleen that she should also follow. He led us toward one of the police cars that sat blocking the driveway.

Another officer, a woman, looked up and put her hand on my shoulder. "You live here?" She asked. I nodded, silently, looking back nervously at the entrance to the apartment and then at her.

"Do you know a young man by the name of Derek?" she asked. Again I nodded.

"Do you know a young woman by the name of Denise?"

The name did not register, so I shook my head.

"Did Derek live here?"

The fact that she used the past tense to refer to Derek struck me forcefully and I couldn't contain my fear. "What's wrong!? What happened to Derek?!" I started yelling, tears coming to my eyes. Colleen grabbed my hand and squeezed it.

"Calm down. Here, sit in the car." She directed me to the back seat of the police cruiser. "Derek has been shot, as has a young woman. We are trying to figure out what happened. Did Derek live here?"

"No," I responded, not quite understanding what I was being told. "He was a friend. He stayed here last night." I was in a panicked daze. Derek and a young woman had been shot? That didn't make any sense. Who would shoot them? Why? I didn't realize that I was actually vocalizing these questions until the woman cop responded, "We're trying to figure that out. Do you know a young man named Kendrick?"

"Is Kendrick OK?!" I was hyperventilating now. I didn't want to hear that Kendrick had been shot as well.

"Yes, he's OK. We'll let you talk to him in just a bit."

IX.

Derek was dead.

He had returned to the apartment after Colleen and I had left. He was high on speed and apparently jealous and angry that Kendrick had slept with both of the girls that they had brought to the party. Kendrick told us that Derek had a pistol when he returned, and that when he came into the living room he started pointing it at him and then at the two girls, yelling about how they were all a bunch of fuckers.

They were that.

Kendrick said that Derek began crying. He wailed about how rejected he felt and how he thought that Kendrick was his friend and how he could not believe that they would do this to him.

And then Derek shot one of the girls in the face.

"It was surreal," Kendrick told me. "It was like time stopped. I couldn't hear anything. I looked at Denise and her face was gone. She was lying there on the floor with her nose missing. I could see the backs of her eyeballs. There was blood everywhere.

Then I heard a ringing sound and I felt like I had fallen backwards into my body. I was looking at Derek. All I could hear was that fucking ringing sound and I was looking at his face. He was crying. He looked at me and said something, but I couldn't hear it. All I could see was his lips moving. All I could hear was that ringing.

And then he said something else and brought the gun up to his own head. I didn't think he would do it, but he did. It shattered his skull. A red spray across the wall and bits of crud all over. His bandana flew off of his head. I didn't know what to do.

I picked up his bandana and started to collect the bone shards that were stuck to the wall and that had fallen onto the ground. I put it all in the bandana. I have it here."

Kendrick had saved the bits of Derek's skull and his brains, wrapped them in his bandana and kept them in a zip-lock plastic bag.

X.

Kendrick was different after Derek's suicide. He became
more detached from others, increasingly suspicious and increasingly
concerned with appearing successful to others. Colleen and I remained
friends with both Kendrick and Richard, but the band broke up, mostly
because Kendrick considered it a childish remnant of our shared
teenage years.

Colleen and I found our own place and moved in together. We
were married ten years later.

CHAPTER ELEVEN: NEUROCYSTICERCSIS

I.

The pain in my stomach continued to worsen. Each visit I made to the doctor resulted in the same advice: avoid late night eating, take antacids as necessary and elevate the head of my bed. The diagnosis of a hiatal hernia was established now, in black and white, in my medical record like some sort of religious truth, and thus no further investigation was necessary.

"There's really nothing to be done," the doctor told me on my last visit to his office, "Unless you want to undergo major surgery. But I really don't think it's necessary. Your symptoms are manageable as they are."

And so it was. The burning sensation remained in the center of my chest, intensifying, as I grew older and older.

II.

The body speaks in its own language; it chatters at us incessantly. The problem is that our minds don't always understand what the body is saying. If our minds could always understand the language of the body, we would be in a state of constant alarm, terrified by the message.

III.

Kendrick stopped by my office at the college. He was in a bad mood, complaining about his boss and his wife.

"I went into work yesterday and my boss gave me this strange look as I walked in the front door. 'Kendrick,' he said, 'I've got a special project for you.' He handed me a file, all the time looking at me with this intense stare. It was like he was scrutinizing me in order to see if I was responding to some drug he had administered. I could tell that he was looking for visible signs of some sort of change in me."

"Maybe he was just looking to see if you had any questions about the new project he had assigned you," I said.

"No, it was more than that. All throughout the day I caught him staring at me. He was checking on me to see how I was acting. I was at my desk in the morning, reading over the new files, and I saw him peering at me over the wall of my cubicle. He didn't even bother to look away when I caught his gaze. You know how a normal person is embarrassed when you catch him staring for too long? A normal person will turn away quickly when you stare back, but yesterday my boss refused to do that. He continued to look at me even when I stared back at him in a challenging way."

"Maybe he was reacting to the way *you* were looking at *him*. Could it be that, perhaps, you were so convinced that he was staring at you that when you returned his stare you reinforced a vicious cycle? Maybe when he first glanced at you it was in an unthinking manner, but when you suspiciously stared back at him he wondered what you were thinking and so he kept staring, and so forth."

"No. That's not how it was. It went on all day long, as if he was expecting to see a change in me. When I came out of the bathroom later in the day he was going in and he looked at me with that same, scrutinizing stare. When I stepped outside for some air, I saw him looking out of the window at me. When I left work for the day, he was walking out to the parking lot behind me, staring."

"Well, you work at the same building, so it's not that surprising that your paths would cross throughout the day."

Kendrick looked annoyed. "But that's not all. When I got home, my wife was giving me the same look. When I walked into the house; when I was making tea in the kitchen; when I came out of the bathroom. Later that night, when I was trying to drift off to sleep, I could tell she was staring at the back of my head!"

After this comment I felt a sense of alarm. Though he never did have much good to say about his boss or his wife(s), I had never before heard him talk as though there was some sort of conspiracy between them.

"Are you trying to say that the two of them are in cahoots?" I asked, the disbelief apparent in my tone.

"*Something* is going on. You didn't see the way they were staring at me. You weren't there. You didn't see the look in their eyes. It was the same look. I'm not imagining this!"

Kendrick was insistent, and of course he was right; I wasn't there and I didn't know what sort of look, what sort of curious, intent stare his wife or his boss had directed toward him. My thoughts on the matter were simply arrived at out of an informal assessment of what my own experience told me was probable. It probably was the case that there was nothing to all of this paranoia because nothing of the sort had ever happened to me. But Kendrick was absolutely convinced that some sort of nefarious scheme was, even as we spoke, being carried out against him, and that both his boss and his wife were somehow involved.

IV.

When I next saw Kendrick, he looked tired, gaunt and sick.

"You look exhausted," I said. I was quite worried, in fact, by the sudden and noticeable change in his appearance.

"I told you; something is going on. I went to the doctor and tried to get him to run some tests. I wanted him to check to see if my boss or my wife had administered some sort of poison to me. He just looked at me the way you looked at me when I first told you about this. He said that I was over reacting. He said that I was over stressed, and so he prescribed some sort of anti-anxiety medication. I think he's in on this, though. I'm not going to take that medicine. I think the doctor, my boss and my wife are trying to kill me!"

The panic in Kendrick's voice was obvious. I had never heard him sound this upset or irrational.

"I've started having terrible headaches. They get so severe that I can hardly think. It's like a fire is burning in the center of my brain, slowly destroying me from the inside out. I'm not sure what I should do. I can't go see a doctor since they're all in on this. I think because my medical insurance is paid for by my work that my boss has been in contact with the doctors. I'm pretty sure that my wife is trying to cash in on the life insurance policy I have through work. It all seems tied back to my job. The only thing I can think to do is to quit and run off to another country where no one knows who I am."

Kendrick had always hated his job, but even for him this was extreme.

"This doesn't make sense, Kendrick," I pleaded with him. "Listen to what you're saying. You really need to go see a doctor. If you are having headaches, this could be something very serious. Why don't you find another doctor, one that has no connection to your work, and have him run some tests?"

Kendrick looked at me with suspicion in his eyes and I knew that there was nothing I could say to convince him I was on his side.

V.

I got a call from Kendrick's wife the next day. Kendrick was in the hospital. He had suffered a massive seizure and remained unconscious in the intensive care unit.

"The doctors have run CT scans and they say he appears to have multiple tumors in his brain."

I was stunned and immediately began to moan in despair and forlornness. I'm afraid I was of no positive use to Kendrick's wife, and in fact my emotional outburst no doubt made her own grief and fear even more intense.

"What happens now?" I blurted out between sobs.

"They're going to operate. They want to go in and remove as many of the tumors as possible."

VI.

The operation took place the following day. I waited with Kendrick's wife at the hospital.

We sat in a cold waiting area for three hours, paging through old issues of uninteresting magazines, while Kendrick underwent brain surgery. My feelings as I sat there were confused and difficult to sort out. There was certainly anxiety and fear, but these were mixed with boredom as well as with a strange animosity toward Kendrick's wife. I kept thinking back to Kendrick's suspicion about her, and I wondered why she had not done something sooner to get him some help. This led me to feel guilty on top of all the other feelings, since I had done no more to help Kendrick than had his wife. I also began to feel guilty about feeling angry toward his wife. This led me to feel angry with myself for feeling guilty about feeling angry.

My feelings went round and round in this fashion until finally a doctor came out into the waiting area with news about the operation. As he approached us I thought I detected an unsettled look in his eyes. It struck me that this was the look of someone who had difficult news, but who was trying to remain impassive and detached. As I thought this, I caught myself also reflecting on Kendrick's suspicious behavior previous to his seizure, and I started to wonder if I myself might have a brain tumor. I then vainly tried to keep myself from thinking about any of this by focusing all of my attention on the doctor and what he had to say.

"Please," the doctor said, "come with me to my office."

We followed him into a small room, furnished with hardly anything other than a large metal desk and large metal filing cabinets. A computer sat atop the surface of the desk. On the walls hung faded, framed pictures of flowers. The framed pictures tilted crookedly this way and that, giving the room a haphazard and thrown together sort of feel. I hoped that this was not indicative of the medical skills of the doctor.

"The operation revealed something that we didn't initially expect," the doctor began. "I'm pleased to tell you that what we found is not cancer. However, it is something quite serious nonetheless. It appears that Kendrick has a condition called neurocysticercsis."

"What does that mean?" Kendrick's wife asked.

"It is a condition in which cysts are formed in the brain due to an infestation of tapeworms. What showed up on the CT scan as tumors are actually liquid filled cysts containing tapeworm larvae."

Neither of us said a word. I cannot even report what I was thinking when I heard this. It was something so unexpected and beyond my realm of understanding that even the confused tumult of my emotions subsided. My mind became a curious blank, and I simply waited to hear more.

"The symptoms that Kendrick experienced were the result of the growth of these larvae in his brain. The condition itself is rather rare, but the symptoms you witnessed are common in cases like this. The cysts, as they grew over a long period of time, interfered with his brain functioning, causing changes in mental processing. His paranoia was the result, followed by the headaches and finally the seizures. During the operation we were able to remove most of the tapeworm larvae, but there are so many of them that we could not get them all. We have some medications that have a very good chance of eliminating the rest of them, and we have begun administering these to Kendrick."

"How the fuck did this happen!?" I exclaimed. "How the fuck did Kendrick get tapeworms in his brain?!"

The doctor waved his hand in an effort to calm my outburst. "Normally this happens when a person eats contaminated or undercooked meat, like pork. The tapeworm eggs are ingested with the meat. They hatch in the gut and then the worms burrow through the stomach lining, get into the bloodstream and eventually travel to the brain where they get lodged and start to grow."

"Is he going to be OK?" Kendrick's wife asked. Her right hand was now spread across her mouth, as if she was protecting herself from inhaling a tapeworm egg.

"We have a great deal of confidence that, yes, he will pull through this. As I said, the medications we are giving him have proven very successful in past cases. We expect that he will recover."

VII.

Kendrick regained consciousness, but remained hospitalized. He stayed in a private room where he received infusions of anti-parasitic medications. I visited him every day, hoping, and expecting, that his condition would improve as time went on. As it turns out, things don't always go as one expects.

Kendrick was alert and talkative when I came to visit, but the content of what he had to say was upsetting in terms of how disconnected it was from reality.

"I'm not sure how I'm going to cope with this change in my career," he said to me the first time I visited him after he regained consciousness. "I mean, I've put so much energy and time into negotiating international peace treaties this past decade that it will be difficult to make the adjustment into medical consulting."

Initially I thought he was joking, so I responded with a humorous remark.

"Oh yeah. The international community is really going to miss you!"

Kendrick looked at me as if I was a pathetic child lacking the capacity to understand the seriousness of what he was talking about.

"You see, the world needs people like me who are able to see past petty national boundaries in order to understand the best interests of humanity as a whole. World leaders tend to be very narrow in how they view reality. They see things from the perspective of their own national interests, often times disregarding what is best for the Earth and for the inhabitants of the Earth overall. In my work this past decade I have been able to break down many of the walls that have separated us as people by demonstrating to presidents and kings that we all share the same vulnerabilities, and that we must strive to adopt a group perspective. We must come to see ourselves as members of one big human family. We must be, as Diogenes stated, cosmopolitans: "citizens of the world." We must put aside our identities as Americans, or Britons, or Russians, or Chinese, or Egyptians, or Iranians in order to realize the unitary oneness of all people."

"So, what have you been doing this past ten years in order to accomplish this?" I asked, spooked both by Kendrick's serious tone and his grandiosity.

"My work has taken me all over the world. I have met with African leaders on the Ivory Coast, convincing them with argument, as well as with the power of my personality, that they must develop the resources of their countries and share the resulting wealth equally with the people who are in need. I have debated issues of morality with the leaders of South America, in the end proving to them that they must work tirelessly to eliminate corruption from their land. Just last year I traveled to Russia, successfully demonstrating to the leaders there that the philosophical foundations of their culture logically imply the need for openness and love of others. This and much more I have been involved with over the past decade."

Kendrick looked at me as if I was a stranger. There was an

arrogant superiority in his gaze that seemed incongruous with the message of brotherhood and equality that he was preaching.

"I've spent a long time trying to show those in power the importance of love, and they have listened. I suppose the success I have had in international relations is what drew me here, to this hospital. I now must teach those in the medical profession how it is that my message will benefit the way they treat and care for patients."

VIII.

Kendrick never left the hospital and he never got better. I visited him every day, and during each visit, his psychosis seemed to increase. On the day of his death, I sat with him for hours as he engaged in a megalomaniacal monologue outlining the success of his life's "work" as the savior of the world.

"I was placed here with a mission," he told me. "Like a worm that eats away at the barriers separating different sections of a garden, in the process bringing life enhancing material and fertilizer to the plants that grow within, I have destroyed the boundaries that separate human beings from one another. I have traveled to all corners of the Earth, and beyond the Earth, creating the connections and conduits through which vital life affirming energies may flow, thus knitting together the universe, making it one and whole again.

We tend to think of ourselves as separate and disconnected. I hope my life work has taught that this is not so. Your separation from others is an illusion that promotes suffering, pain and fear. Think of yourself as interpenetrated with all of the ideas, the influences, the genes and the nutrients that also interpenetrate the rest of the organisms that exist within the universe. You are just one of the connections in which Being grounds itself and gains expression. You are the weigh station, the stop off point at the confluence of various wormholes. The material that floods into you will eventually spill over into others and give them nutrition for growth and prosperity.

Do not close yourself off to others. It is the refusal to see yourself reflected in others that has in the past caused wars and turmoil. I have ushered in a new era of understanding and creative destruction. The postmodernists claimed that diversity was the greatest good; but they were wrong. I have proclaimed the destruction of diversity and the understanding of sameness. This sameness is emptiness; it is nothingness. All of the politicians, all of the professors, all of the experts: they are the same. All of the poor, all of the rich, all of the uneducated, all of the educated: they are the same. They are all nothing. But they are a nothing that may be filled with an ever-flowing substance that enhances the awareness of connectivity. We are all vessels waiting to receive the endowment passed on to us from others. That is all that we are: voidness awaiting the worm.

'Destruction is a creative act'; a great man once wrote words to this effect. He was very wise. He foresaw what I now proclaim. Another great man once said 'When you understand the destruction of all that was made, then you will understand what was not made.' He was very, very wise. What these splendid men understood is what the worm reveals. All life is cultivated in filth, and all filth comes from the passing of life. It is the worm that moves between life and filth, destroying boundaries and allowing for the intermixture of both. The worm creates the hole that makes such intercourse possible. The worm clears the obstruction that keeps life from seeing its source and that keeps the source from seeing its potential in life. The worm encourages the confluence of contents. The worm creates the conditions of fecundity. The worm is love."

Kendrick went on in this vein for hours, and then fell asleep. I left the hospital, and later that night I received a telephone call from his wife telling me that he was dead.

Colleen and I cried together after receiving word of Kendrick's death. We reminisced about him, recalling times past and sharing our memories. We held one another, and said, "I love you," as if this would somehow hold our own deaths at bay. Though Kendrick was close to us both, and though we authentically mourned his passing, we were still more fearful of our own deaths and the end of our own lives together. Kendrick's demise, sad in itself, reminded us that while people close to you may die, no one can die for you. You must always face death for yourself.

IX.

That night I dreamed that I was sitting on an enormous toilet, emptying my bowels into its bowl. I strained and pushed, and with each muscular contraction I could feel more and more shit pass from my body and into the toilet. This went on and on, though in dreamtime it is impossible to say what the actual duration was. It seemed like hours before I felt as though there was nothing left in my colon.

In the dream, I stepped down from the toilet and began to clean myself, however every time I tried to wipe, my hands became smeared with feces. The more that I tried to wipe, the more shit appeared on my hands, and then my arms, and then my body, and then my face. I soon was covered by the brown, mud-like stool, and every move I made simply smeared it further; on the walls, on the floor, on the ceiling.

I decided that I must flush the toilet, but when I operated the lever, more shit came pouring out of the bowl. It appeared as if the plumbing was backed up, and instead of disappearing into the sewer, mountains of shit came bubbling back into the bathroom. I kept flushing the toilet, but more of the brown filth kept spewing forth.

Soon, it was not just shit, but worms and decaying body parts that came flowing out of the toilet bowl. They seethed into the open, riding on a semi-solid matrix of shit, the way that cooking rice rises to the surface of boiling water. More feces carried more worms forward, and the worms ate away at pieces of human ears, penises, toes, nipples, horse hooves, pig noses and dead cat carcasses.

By the end of the dream, I had come to realize it was hopeless to try and flush this all away.

X.

I awoke with a terrified yelp.

Colleen shook me in order to bring me to full consciousness, but for a moment I remained stretched between the world of my dream and the waking world. I was trying to scream, even as I became aware that I was in bed. My body was paralyzed, and I could see human and animal body parts suspended in shit all around me.

"Wake up! You're having a nightmare," Colleen said, shaking me by the shoulders.

Finally I snapped into wakefulness, leaving the awful image of the toilet and the body parts and worms behind. They disappeared in a flash as my body came back under my conscious control.

"How disgusting!" I exclaimed. This remark was made in Colleen's direction, but was not really intended for her. It was, rather, just an expression of visceral disgust.

"Are you alright?" Colleen asked. I could see the concern on her face, and I could hear it in her voice. Come to think of it, I was also able to detect it in the way she shook me awake.

"I had a terrible dream. There was this toilet I couldn't flush. The more I tried, the more shit came pouring out." My gut was in a knot, and that terrible heartburn was upon me. In my chest the burning sensation pulsated and throbbed as if someone had run me through with a flaming sword. My throat was sore and irritated; no doubt from the stomach acid that was seeping into my esophagus from my hiatal hernia. I started to feel nauseous, as if I was on the brink of vomiting.

It was then that Colleen noticed something on my pillow.

"What's that," she said, pointing at a dark spot next to where my head had been lying.

At first glance it appeared as if the dark spot was a stain.

Perhaps I had thrown up a small amount of my stomach contents during the nightmare. But as I inspected it more closely, I could see that the pillow was not stained at all. Rather, it was burned. At the location where my mouth had been opened in a pathetic yelp, the white surface of the pillowcase was charred, as if it had been singed with a blowtorch. Bits of darkened, yet dry, material cracked away from the rest of the pillow, which was largely untouched and normal looking.

"That's fucking weird," Colleen murmured. "How the hell did that happen?"

Chapter Twelve: Stiff Person Syndrome

I.

When I look at a class full of students at the start of each new semester, I am reminded of the tragic reality that all of us will die. Some will die before others, but the undeniable fact of the matter is that everyone is doomed to the same ultimate fate. The younger students will die just as will the older students, and it may happen that many of the older folks will outlive those younger than themselves. Nature is not fair in this way. It doesn't equitably distribute health and prosperity to everyone. Some of us will die young. Some of us will die old. Some of us will die between youth and old age. Nonetheless, all of us will die.

I remember reading that Sidhartha Gautama, before becoming the Buddha, could not look at the young and beautiful dancing girls employed by his father without seeing dancing skeletons. I feel the same way when I look at the youthful faces in class.

Behind all life, no matter how well hidden, death lurks.

II.

Richard told me that my death obsession is illogical.

"There's nothing that you can do about the inevitability of

death," he said. "Becoming depressed and gloomy about death is like wishing for a change in the laws of physics. Your feeling on the matter makes no difference to the way things naturally are, so you might as well just accommodate yourself to reality. Your mother is gone. Kendrick is gone. This is reality."

"It's one thing to say that; it is quite another to carry it through. My question to you is, *how* do I go about changing my feelings? *How* do I move forward? Please, give me some instruction and guidance!"

Richard looked annoyed.

"Look. The biological sciences tell us that negative emotions have developed in us as a survival mechanism. When we feel fear, for instance, it motivates us to run away from a threatening situation, thus allowing us to avoid danger and to live another day. When we feel depression, it encourages us to withdraw from the world around us in order to recuperate so that we can eventually come back to the world and face it with renewed strength. All of these sorts of emotions serve a rational purpose in the struggle for survival.

To allow yourself to be overcome with a persistent fear of death does not serve this same sort of rational purpose. Your obsession with death and mortality is destructive to your well-being. It doesn't help you to avoid danger, since the danger you fear is unavoidable. It doesn't act to give you time for recuperation, since your fear is an obsessive and constant one. All your negativity does is make you unhappy and tedious to be around. Clearly then, it's irrational for you to continue to have these feelings. You need to break this bad habit, put your depressing thoughts to the side and get on with life."

Richard now looked quite pleased. He was entirely satisfied with his argument. The confident, smug expression that he wore on his face was like a challenge. His look said, "Just go ahead and try to prove me wrong," without even uttering any further words.

"I understand your point," I retorted, "but you want to credit nature with causing us to feel what you deem to be 'useful' emotions, and then you want to hold me responsible for choosing to feel what you deem to be 'irrational,' 'unuseful' emotions. I'm not sure that you can have it both ways. If emotional responses are programmed in us by nature, then what is it that leads you to complain that my death obsession is unnatural? By your own account, perhaps we should look more carefully for the probable function that this death obsession of mine might serve. Perhaps there is a survival function that this fear plays in my life. Maybe it encourages me to be extra careful with my health so that I don't expire too soon. Or maybe it makes me think interesting thoughts that others want to read about and discuss, thus making me valuable to others in the world.

According to the biological sciences to which you are making your appeal, whatever exists must have served some sort of function in the struggle for survival; or at the very least it must not have impeded that struggle. Since it is clear that my death obsession exists, I think it follows by your line of reasoning that this obsession has assisted, or at least has not impeded, my survival as an organism; at least up to this point in my life."

Richard got an annoyed look on his face once again.

"It may be the case," he carefully began, "that some emotional responses are due to nature and some are a matter of choice. I would claim that those emotional responses that do serve a rational function are natural, while those that do not serve a rational function are not natural. It is the unnatural emotional responses that you should exert willpower over. Those feelings you should work to eliminate."

I shook my head and responded, "But if any of the emotions we feel are capable of being altered by an act of willpower, then perhaps no emotions are imbued in us by nature. Perhaps even the emotions that you claim are 'rational' are a matter of personal choice. Certainly there are people who overcome some of the natural fears they have about things in the world. They decide that they will change the way they feel about things and set fear aside. So it is that skydivers overcome the 'natural' fear of jumping into a void out of a great height, or soldiers overcome the 'natural' fear of facing violence. Could it be then that no fear is 'natural'? Perhaps we can just pick and choose the things we fear or that we embrace."

Richard sighed. "But the examples you give are of individuals who set fear aside for a purpose. This obsessive death fear of yours doesn't seem to serve any purpose except to make you miserable. I will admit that if there is some purpose that it does serve, then it would make sense to preserve the feeling. If not, I would advise that you work to eliminate the feeling."

"But," I said, "how can you know if it serves a purpose or not while my life is still in the process of unfolding? Your own evolutionary argument suggests that the only way we can know if something actually does serve the purpose of survival is to look backwards over a life already lived and see if that life was helped or hampered, as a whole, by the characteristic under consideration. So, right now you might say that my death obsession is counterproductive because it promotes despair in me. However, suppose I live to be 120 years old, and suppose it was my desire to think about death and despair that drove me to continue living to that age. The conclusion you would have to reach in that case would be that this obsession has actually served me in my struggle for survival."

I smiled broadly at Richard. He just shook his head.

III.

"I miss my mother. I miss Kendrick. I'll miss you when you die as well." I spoke these words to Richard as we sat drinking coffee in a cafe across the street from the college.

"That's supposing that I will die before you. If you die before me, you won't miss me, or anyone, anymore. You'll be gone and there will be no more fears, no more worries and no more anxieties. Does that offer you any comfort?" Richard said, serious and apparently somewhat flattered that I was expressing affection toward him.

"It might if I was able to take up the perspective of a dead person. The problem is that whenever I think about this issue, I have to approach it from the perspective of a living, breathing and feeling human being who is still alive and caught right in the middle of these thoughts. I can't pretend to take up the position of a person who has already died and whose thoughts and feelings have been completely snuffed out. I'm always stuck in the situation of being alive while I'm thinking, and thus I'm still in the situation of anticipating a future that frightens me. All of the intellectualizing in the world can't change the core issue at the root of my nihilism. I fear losing those close to me and I fear no longer being here myself."

Richard just looked at me, saying nothing. I wasn't sure what his silence meant, if it meant anything at all. Perhaps he had no reasonable response to my comments. Perhaps he was just fed up with my whining. Perhaps he agreed with everything I had to say.

Or perhaps he recognized that I was not making an argument anymore. I was simply reporting my feelings. I was honestly telling him about what was going through my head, and this being the case, there was nothing to dispute.

IV.

"Do you remember, when we were younger, when we were in the band, and it seemed as if every other day someone we knew died? There was Billie, who was found hanged in his dorm room at art school. There was Phillip, who died of a heroin overdose. Denise was shot dead by Derek, who then shot himself dead. Jack died in a car crash, and William fell off the roof of a house. Each death was difficult to deal with, but I always had the sense that once we reached a certain age, all of this stupidity would come to an end.

Now that we're middle aged, I'm starting to realize that it never comes to an end. I used to think, if we can just get through this youthful stage of life, things will be different. I thought that once we became middle aged we would all be more stable, more content, more mature. Now I realize that's not the case. When I look at all of the people around me, I don't see well-adjusted, mature adults. I see self-conscious, maladjusted and anxiety-ridden human beings who have no better grasp on the meaning of life than any of us had as kids.

When we were younger, at least we had a sense of friendship and solidarity with one another. When we played shows and when we hung out with our friends, it felt to me we were a part of something. We were punks. We were rebels. Now we've gone our separate ways. We've become different people. Even though some of us are still friends, we don't share the sense of solidarity we once shared. Now we're teachers and lawyers and engineers and computer programmers. When we were young, our individual identities were formed in relation to how different we were from everyone else. We hated the world 'out there,' and so we formed our own subculture as a defense against that world. Now, as middle-aged adults, we form our identities in relation to the role we play within mainstream society. I'm a teacher. I'm paid to teach the children of middle class parents about philosophy. Kendrick was a computer programmer, paid to write programs that make money for a company that sells those programs to the public."

"I'm just unemployed!" Richard interjected, "What does that say about me?"

I chuckled. "My point is, when we introduce ourselves to new people, we tell them what sort of work we do for a living instead of telling them that we're into punk music, or that we're nihilists or anarchists, or that we fear death. We present ourselves to others by describing how useful we are to society rather than by describing what we really feel or believe. And it all seems like a waste of time. It feels as if in growing up we have lost, rather than gained, something."

V.

I began noticing a change in Richard. He had always exhibited shyness, but this shyness started to intensify and he became more and more hesitant to leave his apartment. When I asked him if our recent conversations had become too upsetting, he assured me that this was not the reason for his reclusiveness.

"I've always enjoyed talking with you, but lately I've been finding it harder and harder to think clearly. It's as if I have a single thought that keeps echoing in my head, and every time I try to move past that thought, I get confused. I spend an awful lot of time lately trying to trace everything back to this one idea, and trying to connect everything to it. If I don't do this, it begins to feel as if my head is filled with a bunch of disconnected nonsense. The only way that I can sort things through is by isolating myself and being alone."

"So what is this one thought you keep trying to tie everything back to?" I asked.

"A=A," Richard said.

"A=A?" I asked, perplexed.

"A=A," he repeated. "The Principle of Identity. It's a foundational truth that's absolutely certain and indubitable. It guides all other truths that we articulate in language. When you and I argue about the meaning of life or about the fear of death, I find myself constantly trying to reduce our conversations to this tautology."

"What purpose does this reduction serve?" I inquired.

"I know for certain that the assertion "A=A" is a formal truth. If I'm able to replace each 'A' in this equation with content – for instance 'your fear' equals 'a fear of death' – then I have a firm guide for my thinking. The more complicated our conversations become, the more imperative it is that I carry out this sort of reduction in order to trace out the coherence of our reasoning process. What I've found is that many of our disagreements can be located in a breakdown of logic, and a violation of this rule of identity. Our meanings slip and we tend to equivocate on terms. When this occurs, things get confused and fall apart. By identifying and correcting these slippages in meaning, I'm able to bring everything back to a center that allows me to comprehend clearly and precisely what it is that is at issue."

"That sounds like a potentially useful strategy. Is it working for you?"

"Well, lately I have been unable to move very far from this principle. It seems that I'm increasingly unable to make the necessary reductions. The world is just becoming more and more illogical, it seems."

VI.

I hadn't heard from Richard for quite some time. He wasn't answering his telephone, and I wasn't receiving any responses by email. I decided to drop by his apartment one afternoon to check up on him.

After ringing his doorbell, it was about three minutes before he appeared. I waited because I could hear him moving around inside, shuffling slowly toward the front door. He even called out in a weak, hoarse voice, "Just a minute!" When he did appear at the door, he looked very stiff and rigid; as if his arms and legs were locked into position. His shoulders were hunched up around his neck and when he moved it looked as if his joints were not bending.

"Richard? What's wrong?" I asked immediately upon seeing him in this condition.

"Come on in and I'll tell you," he responded, peering warily at the street outside. He looked unusually vulnerable and eager to retreat back inside.

I followed Richard as he climbed the stairs leading from the front door to his apartment. Each step looked like an ordeal in itself. He held onto the handrail with both of his hands and swung his legs to the side and up, never bending his knees or his hip joints as he moved. As he climbed each step, this awkward, stiff legged movement was repeated until, after another three or four minutes, we were finally at the top of the short flight of stairs. If I was not so concerned about his well-being, the sight might have been comic. He had the appearance of someone who had, perhaps, worked out too vigorously at the gym the previous day, painfully straining his muscles. However, knowing Richard, this was highly unlikely. Strenuous physical exercise was certainly not on the list of his usual activities.

Once we finally got inside his apartment, Richard fell backwards, stiff as a board, onto a mattress that lay in the middle of the one room that served as both his living- and his bedroom. He lay there with his eyes closed and said nothing.

"My joints are stiffening up, and my doctor thinks it's all in my head," Richard spoke, his eyes still closed as he lay on the mattress.

"Well, I can see that it's not *all* in your head," I responded.

Richard opened up one of his eyes and looked at me. "There's something *physically* wrong," he began, "and the doctor just won't take the time to investigate. He referred me to a psychiatrist who wants me to start taking some kind of antidepressant medication. He diagnosed me with something he calls 'stiff person syndrome.'"

"I've never heard of that," I said.

It's a condition in which a person becomes progressively stiffer and stiffer over time. The mainstream medical community claims it has no physical basis, but that it is, rather, related to depression. They really don't understand it, but they say there's no treatment. Eventually, sufferers just become completely rigid. They can't move at all."

Richard looked at me with a hint of fear in his eyes.

"This is *physical!*" he insisted, and then closed his eyes once again.

VII.

Richard's condition got worse and worse. It got to the point where he couldn't leave his apartment and he had to have nurses feed and bathe him. I'd periodically visit him in the afternoons after I left campus. Each time I saw him, not only was his body more and more rigid, but his thinking process seemed progressively to deteriorate. He seemed to get stuck on a particular point and then would be unable to let that point go, repeating and rephrasing what he had already stated over and over again.

"My condition is physical," he began on this one particular day. "It is physical. Physical is not mental. The physical is non-mental, but that doesn't mean that the non-mental is always physical. Non-physicality is an attribute of the mental, but it does not exhaust its essence. The physical, on the other hand, is always not non-non-mental. The attribute of being not non-non-mental is always an attribute of physicality. Being not non-non-mental is equivalent to not being mental. The physical is not mental. A=A.

The doctors want me to believe that my physical condition is the result of my mental condition. This is impossible. The physical is not mental. If something is the cause of something else, it must somehow interact with that in which it produces an effect. But if two substances are completely distinct in their essences, then it is impossible for those substances to interact. The physical and the mental are distinct from one another in their essences. The physical is not mental. Therefore the physical cannot have an effect on the mental and the mental cannot have an effect on the physical. The mental is non-physical. The physical is non-mental. A=A.

If all of this is so, then my condition must find its cause in something other than the mental. If the condition is a physical condition, then it must have a physical cause. Only the physical can affect the physical. A=A.

Therefore, my thoughts are completely distinct from my physical body. They have no effect on my body and my body has no effect on my thoughts. What I think has nothing to do with my condition. The state of my body has nothing to do with the nature of my thoughts. A=A.

The medication that the doctors are giving me is physical. Therefore it cannot have an effect on my thought process. Therefore, it cannot change my thought process. If the doctors want to claim that my way of thinking is the cause of my physical condition, they are, then, involved in a double contradiction. First, the mental cannot affect the physical. Second, physical medication cannot affect thoughts. The physical is not the mental. The mental is not the physical. A=A."

I sat and listened to Richard proceed through this deduction, and then repeat the deduction at least four times that afternoon.

VIII.

When I next visited, Richard was in an even more disabled state. I entered his room to find him, rigid as a board, lying on his back with his arms at his sides and his legs stretched out straight.

"Hi Richard. How are you doing today?" I asked.

"I am Richard. Richard is I. A=A."

"I am feeling bad. Badness is being felt by me. A=A."

And then he began to repeat "A=A" for the next hour.

IX.

Eventually Richard's body became so rigid that his lungs and his heart stopped moving. Shortly before his death, the only words that came out of his mouth were "A=A."

Richard was buried in a cemetery overlooking the ocean. Only a handful of people attended the funeral. Colleen and I were there for a short period of time and we had the opportunity to offer our condolences to Richard's mother and his sister.

"He was a brilliant man," I said to Richard's mother. "He was one of the smartest people I've ever met."

"Well, thank you," she responded. "I just don't understand how all of this happened. He was always troubled, ever since he was a child, but we tried to help him all that we could. He always wanted to be certain about things. He was never satisfied with just accepting the uncertainty of life and moving on. I just hope he's in some place better now. I hope he's some place where all of that uncertainty and sadness have been swept away."

"I'm sure he is," I said. Even as these words were coming out of my mouth, I regretted saying them. I wasn't sure at all.

At that very moment, I realized, Richard's body was undergoing radical change. It was decaying and disappearing. The earth was reclaiming his constituents, and the unique individual that we all knew and cared for was slowly disintegrating into nothing.

Toward the end of his life, Richard had striven to reach a point of unchanging certainty. In his death, he now entered into the irreversible changes that accompany bodily decomposition.

His body was betraying his mind.

X.

That night I dreamed I was made of glass. In the dream, I was trying to keep myself from thinking any thoughts, because I knew that as these thoughts moved around inside of me, their violence would eventually shatter my body. The more I concentrated on stopping my mind from thinking, however, the more agitated I became until an awful, terrible feeling of doom overcame me.

I woke up from the dream just as my glass body was shattering into millions of pieces.

CHAPTER THIRTEEN: RECURRENCE

I.

In mourning Kendrick and Richard, and in trying to come to terms with their bizarre deaths, I became overwhelmed with issues and fears fundamental to my nihilistic distress. Losing close friends was bad enough in itself, but with their passing I was also reminded of my mother's death, and this reinforced my more general anxiety about the finite and transitory nature of all things. Nothing is permanent. The world is absurd. All is fire.

Richard, before his death, had suggested to me that there is something immature and overly dramatic in my fixation on these ideas. We all have to deal with the passing of loved ones, and we must all confront death periodically throughout life, but it does no good to become obsessed with these thoughts. Everyone is in the same boat. Everyone dies. It's better just to direct one's attention toward the positive things in life and to enjoy the time that we have. Be realistic. Don't be depressing. All of this has been said to me, and it is easy to say such things.

But just saying these things doesn't change the fact of the matter. The world, and everything in it, is doomed to destruction. How can I enjoy my life when meaningless oblivion is just around the corner? All things lose their luster when I think about this fact. My education, my philosophy, my house, my job; all of these things seem like silly distractions from the reality of death.

II.

Years of teaching have granted me the opportunity to see successive waves of students pass through my classroom, and with each new semester I recall the time when I too was a new college student at this very same campus. It was a time when the threat of death was not as prominent in my mind as was my desire to find direction and meaning in life. I detect this same desire in many of the students who cycle through my classes.

I'm afraid, however, that philosophy will always fail to produce final and comforting answers about the meaning of life, just as it always fails to offer final and satisfying answers to the fears I have about death. Nonetheless, in encouraging us to think about and discuss our concerns, philosophy is edifying in its own unique way. It helps to clarify what we believe, what we hope for and what we fear. It encourages us to put our thoughts in order and to understand the structure of our conceptual world.

II.

Students come and go. They appear in my classes, I form relationships with them, and then they graduate, moving on to other things. For a short period we share our time with one another and then we go our separate ways. In all of this I once again see impermanence; the only lasting thing in our world.

And yet, while particular individual students are constantly changing over time, I have come to realize that there is a degree of regularity in the general types and kinds of students that I encounter. It is as if each unique, actual, concrete student is the embodiment of a certain number of recurrent ideal types that appear again and again. Without realizing it, these students express the same thoughts, the same perspectives and the same concerns as some other set of students that came before them.

For instance, there is the hard-headed philosophy student who is confident that the proper use of logic and reason is adequate to distinguish truth from error. This type of student usually expresses him or herself in a tight-lipped and confident fashion, mirroring in speech the formal structure of an argument that moves systematically from premises to conclusion. All issues are matters of logic, according to this type, and all questions can be resolved using the proper logical tools.

There is also the student mystic who is attracted to philosophy because he or she sees it as a way to contemplate the mysteries of reality without the dogmatic demands of an institutionalized religion. This type of student is apt to express him or herself by making appeals to inner feelings and experiences, using intuition rather than logic as a guidepost in discussion.

Then there is the enthusiast. This type of student is excited about everything that philosophy has to offer. Even the most depressing thinkers are viewed by this kind of individual as magnificent and wonderful. All philosophical systems are true to the enthusiast, even though many of those systems contradict one another. What is important, so the enthusiast seems to believe, is that people communicate and express themselves. What people say is not so important as the fact that they say something.

But there is also the skeptic. Whereas the enthusiast accepts everything, the skeptic finds problems with all philosophies. No one has ever spoken the truth according to this type of student. This type is drawn to philosophy because of what he or she regards as its critical power. Philosophy for the skeptic is a tool useful for dismantling nonsense, but it has no positive capacity to articulate the truth. Usually this sort of student sits well to the back of the classroom, remaining quiet until there is some point or issue to be disputed and shown to be fallacious.

These are among the ideal types of students who cycle through each section of each semester of classes. In each of them I see a reflection of my friends and loved ones, as well as a bit of myself.

III.

Student clothing fashions, too, recur. When I was a student at this same school, I adopted the punk rock style and now, many years later, the fashion of my youth has reemerged. Again there are punk rockers on campus, as well as hippies and skinheads and mods. They all look familiar, but each also possesses something unique to the times. The fashions are a mixture of old and new. They retain recognizable elements from the past, but many of these elements have been exaggerated and amplified.

When I was a youth, it was shocking to put a safety pin through your cheek. Compared to today's piercings, that's tame. Today everything is pierced: tongues, eyebrows, noses, lips and even spare flesh on the neck.

When I was a youth, some of my friends had a few tattoos, most of which were homemade. Today, students are covered from head to foot in elaborate and expensive tattoos of very high quality.

A student in one of the philosophy classes confided in me one day, saying, "My generation hasn't done anything new. We've taken everything from past generations and just mixed it all together. Our style of dress, our music and our artwork is just a rehash of past culture."

I remember thinking the same thing about my own generation. What is always unique, however, is the boldness and audacity with which each youthful cohort forcefully expresses itself.

IV.

Nietzsche echoed the sentiments of the ancient Greek Stoics when he proclaimed the eternal recurrence of all things. Nothing is new. All things have been done before. Everything in the universe repeats again and again. This conclusion follows logically from two premises that are widely accepted today:

A) The universe is made of a finite amount of material substance.

B) Time unfolds infinitely.

If A and B are true, then it must follow that everything that happens in the history of the universe will reoccur again and again. Over an infinite amount time, a finite amount of material substance will exhaust its possible combinations. If this is the case, then the patterns of the universe must repeat themselves infinitely.

So while each and every particular thing is impermanent, every particular thing in the universe embodies a pattern that will repeat again and again into infinity. Is there any comfort to be found in this insight? Nietzsche thought so.

Patterns bring familiarity, which in turn brings comfort.

V.

One of the greatest joys lost to me as an adult is the feeling of oneness and unity I felt with other punk rockers when I was a youngster. Punk clubs were our temples, the music our means of worship, and rebellion was our religion.

From an outsider's perspective, punk shows appeared to be pure chaos. I remember one particular evening when our band was playing and the owner of the club became alarmed at what he perceived to be a riot waiting to happen. Because of an injury sustained to my head, I had a wound that was dripping blood down the side of my face as I sang. Covered in sweat and blood, screaming into the microphone, throwing my body here and there across the stage, I must have appeared to him like some sort of out of control maniac. The audience was a mass of writhing bodies with no respect for the distinction between stage and dance floor. I became engulfed as they moved, jumped and thrashed about, sharing the microphone with me and singing along. As a participant, the experience was exhilarating. As a detached spectator, it was, apparently, alarming. We were in the midst of a mystical frenzy.

The owner of the club on this particular evening panicked. From the accounts of those who were in a position to observe him I learned that he began to shout and scream for the show to come to an end. This, of course, was a vain gesture, considering the momentum of the performance and the participation of the crowd. When he came to realize this, the owner started to scream "I hate violence!" and "I will not tolerate violence in my club!" Upon uttering this he proceeded, systematically, to take the dishes from behind the counter and to smash them on the floor, one by one.

VI.

Repeatedly, shows would be broken up early in the evening by the police who always found some reason to intervene, either because of noise complaints, lack of permits, or suspiciously vague laws concerning curfews. Sometimes the shows self-destructed without any outside help.

One evening we were playing at a party held on a farm in a rural area quite some distance from the city. Our band was set up in a barn on the back lot of the property. The audience was densely packed, and there was no stage. Everyone was on the same level, gathered together and socializing among bales of hay and bags of livestock feed. We launched into our first number, "Nihilist Void," a song that expressed feelings about the absurd meaninglessness of life:

"Vision clouded by some unnamed drug,
Gestures ignored with an apathetic shrug.
Feelings not felt until they're analyzed,
This must be what it's like to be lobotomized.

Then with one disruption there is no more silence,
It's shattered by adrenaline and blind, cold violence.
There is no other choice but let it take control,
And be consumed by action, body and soul.

It seems so important as you do what you do,
But in times to come no one remembers you.
Your actions are forgotten and your feelings destroyed.
You've become one with the nihilist void.

Your body is a symbol of futility.
Hands that can't feel, eyes that can't see.
Legs that won't take you where you want to go,
And a brain that can't comprehend what you want to know.

We strive for perfection, though we don't have the tools.
We're less like human beings; more like pack mules.
The baggage that we carry is a heavy load,
And our journey only takes us on a dead-end road.

It seems so important as you do what you do,
But in the times to come, no one remembers you.
Your actions are forgotten and your feelings destroyed.
You've become one with the nihilist void."

    As the song came to an end, a gang of about six skinheads entered the barn. The individuals themselves were all familiar and generally friendly one on one, but when gathered together in a group this large, trouble was sure to follow. We had seen this happen again and again.

    Before the band could launch into another song, one of the

skinheads yelled at Kendrick, "You stupid faggot!"

Kendrick immediately responded, "Fuck you, stupid skinhead!" and that was enough provocation for things to fall apart. The skinhead advanced on Kendrick and Kendrick advanced on the skinhead. As they moved toward one another, a crowd of us tried to intervene by getting in between them. This served to provoke the skinhead gang also to advance, and before anyone even had time to think about what was happening, a brawl was in progress.

Arms, legs, torsos, heads; all of these body parts moved this way and that, smashing into one another with no real planning or calculation. From the outside, it must have looked like slam dancing. From inside the mass of colliding bodies, however, everything was pandemonium and desperation. Once this many people were packed together, they all became subject to the brute laws of physics.

In the midst of this melee, I grabbed onto one of the skinheads, thinking that my weight would be sufficient to pull him to the ground. From behind, I threw my arms around his neck and then jumped onto his back. To my surprise, he shouldered my body as if I was a backpack, and continued to punch and fight his way through the crowd. I hung on, thinking that eventually he would tire and fall, but because he was so large, I seemed to have no effect on his ability to fight.

Kendrick appeared and began throwing punches at the skinhead upon whose back I was riding. While he struck his intended target a number of times, my face also suffered a good deal of abuse, as it was peeking out from behind the skinhead's shoulder. Finally, one of his punches landed squarely in my face, and at that point I released my grip and fell to the ground.

From the ground, the confusion and turmoil continued. I landed, face down, on top of another body, and then someone else landed on top of me. I was pinned, unable to move, and staring at the back of someone's bald head. I had no idea if this person was a member of the gang or if it was one of our friends. I recall yelling in frustration, and as I did so I tried unsuccessfully to free myself from the dogpile. It was no use.

The head that was directly below me, and at which I was forced to stare, now became the target of repeated abuse. It was a strange, fragmented view of the situation I shall now describe, but it is all that I can honestly say I witnessed. First, I saw a glass beer bottle come down on the back of the head. The bottle bounced off of the top of the skull with no apparent damage done. Then another, larger bottle, probably a wine bottle, came arcing down. It struck the back portion of the head, landing just about an inch from my watching eyes. Upon impact, a torrent of blood exploded from the scalp, splattering my face and everything else in the immediate vicinity. I struggled to free myself anew, but still I was trapped in place. Then fists came raining down on the bleeding and battered head. Some of the fists were wearing sharp rings; rings in the shapes of skulls and bats and vicious tiger heads that tore further into the back of the head trapped below me. By the time the blows ceased, I was staring at a mass of raw, red and bleeding flesh.

I heard a voice yell, "Get the fuck off of me!" It was the skinhead who had initiated the fight.

Someone grabbed me by the back of my shirt and pulled me up. The dogpile dispersed and the skinheads, as a group, retreated out the front door of the barn. I learned later that as they departed, the gang smashed out the windshields of all of the cars sitting parked in the driveway.

VII.

Similar patterns repeat themselves.

I'm certain, as I survey the young faces gathered together in this philosophy class, that these types of dramas continue to be played out today. On my left sits a group of students dressed in punk rock fashion. There is a young man with a blue mohawk whispering to his girlfriend, who is dressed in a Sex Pistols t-shirt. She has multiple facial piercings and arms covered in elaborate tattoos of skulls, anarchy signs, and flames. Their friends sit around them, forming a distinctive presence within the classroom.

On the other side of the classroom sits a smaller number of hippie students, sporting long hair and not wearing any shoes. They are more quiet and attentive than the punk rock students.

A lone skinhead sits front and center, his attention completely focused on me as I speak. This young man has been in many of the philosophy classes, and though I have seen him socializing outside of class with others wearing his style of dress, I have never seen him interact with any of the students in class. His head is shaved, he wears tall Dr. Marten boots, suspenders that dangle around his waist, and a Fred Perry sports shirt. Around the base of his throat is tattooed a series of dashes, the words "Cut Here" following the curve of the line as it circles his neck.

All of these students are young and eager to talk about philosophy. They all want to figure out the meaning of life. All of them could be transported back in time, to this same room in this same college, and I imagine that if that was to happen, I would be among them, not as their instructor, but as their peer.

VIII.

I dreamed the word "TRAGEDY." In the darkness of my mind's movie theater, the letters making up this word appeared, and as I slept, I contemplated the meaning of the concept signified by the word.

In tragedy, a character makes choices and carries out actions that result in calamity and destruction. The tragic figure is consumed by the calamity, in the end coming to recognize his or her own role in bringing about the dreadful chain of events. While tragedy results in suffering and torment for the protagonist, there is something redemptive about the suffering. In the experience of tragedy, a human being comes to understand himself and to accept responsibility for the choices he has made.

Human life is tragic. Even though we are unable to foresee all of the consequences that will ultimately result from our actions, we must accept responsibility for our choices and embrace the terrible consequences that sometimes follow as the risks that are necessary to living life fully and authentically. Life is tragedy.

IX.

When I woke up in the morning, these thoughts stayed with me. As I drove to work, I could not get the word "TRAGEDY" out of my thoughts. The word echoed through my mind as I walked into my first class of the day. There, sitting alone, front and center in the classroom, was the young skinhead. He was wearing a T-shirt that stopped me in my tracks. Across the chest of his shirt, in large, black letters, was the word "TRAGEDY."

"Where did you get that shirt?" I asked as I stood there, astounded.

"I bought it at a show. It is the name of one of my favorite bands."

X.

There is no such thing as progress or regress. The world is not getting better and better, nor is it getting worse and worse. It is simply moving along into the future, reiterating in different configurations the patterns that have already occurred. We can't help but play a role in this unfolding drama, but it is a mistake to think that what we do makes any difference to the grand scheme of things.

Chapter Fourteen: Spontaneous Human Combustion

I.

The longer I live, the more acutely aware I become that I am also constantly dying. Day-to-day activities and distractions only serve to mask the underlying and chronic awareness that I am on my way toward oblivion; that there will be a point in time at which I no longer am here. This is one of the patterns in life that repeats endlessly.

Each funeral I attend drives this point home with greater and greater force. Gathering together in groups to mourn the passing of another human being – my mother, my coworkers, my friends – grief reminds me of the one overwhelming fact that I would like to forget and cover over. We all are dying.

Perhaps there is some consolation in the understanding that we are all in this together, that there is nothing personal about the whole thing. Everyone dies and so when we do speak of such things, everyone knows what we are feeling and dreading.

But maybe it is this anxiety over death that separates us from one another, making us so unique that no one can understand anyone else. Sometimes I feel as if I stand alone with my fear, dread and anxiety.

When I speak about it, I am seen as morbid. I am silenced with looks telling me such topics are indecent. Most people would prefer not to be reminded of mortality. "Why not be grateful for the life you've been given?" I ask myself the same question. Why can't I be grateful? I don't know.

Though all of us are mortal and thus will die, no one can die for us. Though all of us are mortal and thus anticipate death, no one can force us to confront this reality. Though all of us are mortal, we are all alone when it comes to facing our deaths.

The thought that I will at one point no longer be here, that I will evaporate into nothingness never again to exist, drives me to nihilism. This one fact of death makes everything else in life meaningless.

II.

One of the distractions that I began to pursue as an adult in order to divert my attention from the looming inevitability of death was running. It is not that I particularly enjoy running itself, but rather that when I run, my physical state is such that depression becomes an impossibility. The movement of my limbs, the force of my breathing, the pumping of my blood and the release of various hormones and chemicals puts my body into a state incompatible with the mental condition of gloominess. It is the mindlessness of running that makes it therapeutic. When I run, all of my attention becomes focused on the physics of the activity, and over the course of an hour, this draws the mind far away from the worries and anxieties that are part of anticipating the future and its bleak inevitability. When running, I find that I must focus on the "now," and in this I become quite stupid. I stop philosophizing, I stop pondering, I stop *thinking* altogether. I simply move.

The philosopher Schopenhauer found something similar in listening to music. In music, he was swept away into a phenomenon that absorbed his attention so completely that all of the anxiety and dread of normal existence was forgotten momentarily. In the rhythms and the harmonies of a musical performance, Schopenhauer claimed to have discovered the closest thing to bliss that a living, breathing, human being can ever experience. Past and future concerns melted away, he claimed, as his mind became enraptured in the moment. His individual will, it seemed, was swept away into the collective will of the universe for the duration of a song's performance, and during this period of time he felt a sense of unity and oneness with the world. It is misleading to say that the experience itself had duration, for Schopenhauer's point is that all sense of time stops during the joyous experience of music, and thus all worries about death cease to exist. As the mind rides the rhythms of music, it settles into a meditative state of contentment that is free of past or future preoccupations. It resonates in the moment, reposing in the here-and-now.

The problem is, as Schopenhauer himself points out, no musical performance goes on forever.

Likewise, no run can go on forever.

Nonetheless, running does serve, in my case, as a temporary break from the chronic anxiety that is involved in contemplating mortality. Some people listen to music, some people get involved in politics, some people have important jobs as CEO's of large corporations, some people take drugs or drink. I run. Running is my adult replacement for punk rock music.

In a way, I think running works for me particularly well now because of what I see as its symbolic appropriateness. The music aficionado, in cultivating his tastes, might be tempted to develop a high opinion of his own level of culture. The politician might be tempted to think of himself as doing public good as he works in government. The CEO, in exercising his influence, might maintain the illusion of his own power and importance. Drug addicts and alcoholics, as they hang out with one another and share their poisons, might be distracted by a culture of hipness and connection to other addicts. All of these pretensions seem, to me, somehow dishonest. On the other hand, as a runner I frankly embody and display my motivation in the very act of doing what I do. I'm not foolish enough to think that I'm developing any great capacity in myself or that I'm striving for Olympic gold. I run simply to forget. I'm running *away* from my despair.

III.

The places where I choose to go running vary according to my mood and motivation.

I find that I am particularly distracted from death when I run in nature; in the hills and forests near where I live. I suspect that the strenuousness of these runs forces my body into a state of singular concentration. Climbing hills, navigating fallen tree branches and hopping around streams keeps my mind focused on the physical terrain to such a degree that abstract thoughts about mortality are not permitted access to consciousness. Running in these surroundings is especially invigorating as a result. Upon completing one of these runs I feel as if I have just awakened from a deep sleep. The awful world is still there to greet me as I leave the trail, but I am nevertheless rested and better able to cope with all of its horrible details.

The drawback of running in nature, however, is that it takes an extra charge of motivation to get myself to begin the run in the first place. Because of the unique demands that a nature trail puts on the body, the mind is prone to antecedent exhaustion as it anticipates the physical demands to come. Thus, I find myself making excuses for why it is that I don't have the time to go on such runs, or why it is better for me to just run on the street, or on the treadmill at the gym. Running in the hills, after all, is regularly accompanied by muddy shoes, the need to apply sunscreen, the need to get into the car and drive to a trailhead, etc. The entire procedure can become overwhelming even before it gets started.

On the other hand, running on the street takes very little preparation. To run on the street, all I need to do is put on my running clothes and walk out of the front door. I've found that I can motivate myself to embark on such a run on the spur of the moment. I need hardly anything at all in order to get started; just a momentary inclination and the bodily ability to walk outside.

The drawback of running on the street is that such runs rarely result in the degree of distraction that I experience when in nature. On the street, runs are less physically taxing and so my mind is much more free to wander and to reflect on the sorts of dark and distressing thoughts that I would prefer to forget. On the street there are no fallen logs, no bends in the trail, no diverted streams to dodge. There is pavement and perhaps an occasional pedestrian to avoid. I find that under these circumstances not only is my mind freed to ponder the familiar old worries and fears, but it also becomes obsessed with the tediousness of the run itself. My mind vacillates back and forth between the stupidity of running in a straight line down a concrete sidewalk and the idea that my life is one big, sad and absurd joke. The run itself becomes a metaphor representing everything else in my life. It is a pointless exercise leading nowhere.

I don't mean to overstate the issue. Insofar as running on the street forces me to focus on a physical activity, it does break into and interrupt my obsessive death awareness, and thus it is somewhat therapeutic. It does not, however, do so to the same degree as a nature run.

Even less satisfying is the sort of running that takes place on a treadmill at the gym. The technology of the treadmill transforms the primal act of running into a quantifiable, precise and sanitized activity. With the treadmill, even less preparation is required than running on the street, yet the cost of this convenience is an experience of pure tedium. You stare at yourself in a mirror as the minutes tick away right in front of your eyes. You monitor the calories you have burned, the imaginary distance you have traveled and the terrain you have traversed, all of which are displayed digitally. You may even decide to intervene as you are running and change the slope of the hill you wish to climb, the speed at which the belt is spinning, or the level of strenuousness at which you are working. You find yourself in total control of the event, and because of this, it is impossible to lose yourself in the experience. You are constantly aware and thinking and choosing and calculating. You are like a rat that is running its own experiment on itself.

While running by its very nature forces the body into a physical condition of stress, thus encouraging the mind to drift away from abstract worries about the future, the various places that one runs can either heighten or lessen this tendency. For my own purposes, I gain the most benefit from running out of doors, on trails that snake through the wilderness.

IV.

Running in nature robs you of your ego by making your body an extension of the landscape. Like water in a stream, you flow along the trail. You become crooked as the path bends.

V.

One of my favorite nature runs takes me on a path through the countryside along the bayside waterfront. This trail is particularly strenuous as it involves the ascent and descent of some very steep rises and valleys. As this path winds its way next to the bay, it takes me through open grassland, forested areas and finally to the top of a knoll that overlooks the blue water below. During this run I commonly encounter herds of deer grazing in meadows, flocks of wild turkeys, squirrels, and various other wildlife. These creatures, whose expected life spans are so much shorter than my own, bring me a strange sort of comfort. Here they are, doing what animals do, with no concern about the meaning of existence or the absurdity of the world.

As I approach these animals, they run away, seeing in me a threat to their lives. Like me, they reflexively flee from death. Unlike them, however, I am always fleeing, even in my most placid moments. Deer, turkeys, squirrels and other animals flee only when a threat is physically immanent. I, on the other hand, am in perpetual flight from death.

VI.

On this particular day, my run starts out perfectly.

The sun beats down on my body and warms me. Almost immediately I begin to sweat. My face and torso become covered with perspiration that mixes with the sunscreen on my skin, creating a creamy mess that drips off the tip of my nose and down my stomach. As I come around a bend in the path, a gust of wind blows and cools my body temperature instantly. A chill goes through me; but it is not unpleasant. It is a sensation that makes me feel vital and alive in the moment.

The sensations that I experience are detached from any sort of lasting intellectual reflection. As I continue to run, I experience fluctuations in body temperature, the pounding impact as my feet hit the dirt, the breeze as it either blows in my face or on my back. As all of this transpires, it registers on a mental level only at the very instant of its occurrence. There is no anticipation on my part. I have no worries about what is to come, nor any regrets about what has been. As I run I exist in a virtually timeless "now" with no past or future.

And yet I *must* retain some sense of time somewhere, tucked into the recesses of my mind. How else would I know when I am halfway through the run? How else could I foresee that at the end of the trail I will pause long enough to survey the bay water below and then turn around to run back in the opposite direction? I am certainly aware of these temporal details, but still, as I am engaged in this act of running, I feel liberated from the usual, everyday experience of time. In particular, I don't think about the long-term trajectory of my life as a whole. Because I am engaged in the relatively mindless task of stupidly running from one end of this dirt path to the other, I am granted the luxury of simply being in the moment as defined by the length of this activity. I am only thinking about running.

The Germans have a term they use in order to refer to the moment. They call it *Augenblick*, which means "blink of an eye." While even the blink of an eye consists of a duration, it is of such a short duration that practically speaking we think it instantaneous. Perhaps this is what is so precious about my experience as I run. It is as close as I can get to existence within the blink of an eye.

VII.

I am running. Warmth. Salty perspiration. Heavy breath. Cool breeze. Difficult hill.

And then, pain.

The pain is a burning, searing jolt that originates in my stomach and shoots both upwards and downwards. It singes a path up my throat and down to my anus simultaneously, in the "blink of an eye." In the blink of an eye I have shit my pants. In the blink of an eye I have vomited on the trail in front of me.

I stop running, but the pain only increases in intensity. It feels as if my insides are about to burn away to cinders. I lay down on the ground, hoping that the discomfort will subside, but it only seems to get worse and worse. I vomit again and I void my bowels a second time.

The fact that there is no one else on the trail is both a blessing and a curse. It is a blessing because I am now self-consciously aware that I am covered in shit and puke. I don't want anyone to see me like this. On the other hand, it is a curse because I'm not sure that I can make it back to my car without some sort of assistance. The pain has become overwhelming and I don't feel capable of doing anything other than lying on the ground. So that's what I do; I lie there, the filth from both ends of my body mingling in a puddle beneath me.

VIII.

The pain wrenches me out of the instant, thrusting me back into the world of everyday time. I am uncomfortable, self-conscious and calculating my next move. How will I get back home? What if someone sees me? What is wrong with me? Am I going to die?

My first move is to take off my running shorts and my underwear. I clean myself as best I can, toss the soiled underpants into the foliage next to the trail and slip my shorts back on. Next, I stand up in order to see how steady I am on my feet. I am more in control of my body now, rising to my full height. The burning pain has started to subside and I no longer feel as if I will lose control of my bowels.

I start walking back toward the car, slowly at first and then more quickly as I gain confidence that my bout of vomiting and shitting has come to an end. I have made it almost the entire way to the car when that same burning pain reoccurs, except that this time it is centered near my heart. I grasp my chest as the sensation of hotness becomes ever more severe. Am I having a heart attack?

I continue to walk toward the car, and as I do so there is an intense feeling of heat on the palms of my hands. I pull them away from my chest and I am stunned at what I see.

My hands are on fire.

Panicking, I once again fall to the ground and roll about in the dirt. I do this because it is ingrained in my mind that one should "drop and roll" when on fire. However, since it is only my hands that are in flames, this maneuver accomplishes little more than to start a small blaze in the grass next to the path. Realizing this, I slap the dirt on the trail with open palms, hoping this will extinguish my hands. It works, and within seconds, they are no longer on fire.

I stand up, remove my hat and swat at the blaze that has started in the grass. It seems to go out quickly and I hope that it is extinguished for good.

My hands look swollen. I realize this is because they are now severely blistered and red. They look grotesque and fragile, as if they might pop at the slightest disturbance. I'm afraid that if that happens, all of the skin will slough off and I'll be left with a pair of raw, fleshy and vulnerable claws.

I start to walk quickly toward the car again, my arms held out in front of me, palms facing upwards. I imagine that I must look like some sort of zombie as I shamble forward, injured, filthy and disoriented.

And then the pain in my chest begins again.

I walk more quickly, hoping to get to my car before another attack comes fully upon me. I don't want to move too fast, however, since I am worried about falling and having the skin of my hands peel off like a couple of flimsy gloves. Step by step I move ahead, moaning both with pain and with a sense of my own pathetic vulnerability.

I'm almost there when the burning in my chest literally erupts and I see two jets of blue flame shoot out of my nipples. The fiery jet originating from my left nipple is about 5 inches in length, while the one originating from my right nipple reaches to about twice that distance. There is a loud sound, like the "whooshing" noise made by a blowtorch, which accompanies this unusual display. Both flames continue to burn for about ten seconds before they abruptly subside.

I have stopped walking and am standing still, about twenty feet away from my car. My arms are still stretched out in front of me and I am looking down at my own upper body. There are two bald, singed circles in my chest hair; one nipple in the center of each. Both nipples are severely blistered and red, even worse than my hands. It looks like I have two broken and barbequed cherry tomatoes attached to my chest.

The internal burning pain in my torso has passed, but it has now been replaced by another sort of pain located externally, on the surface of my hands and my nipples. Both areas of my body feel fragile and damaged. I fear that any sudden movement will tear open the skin and expose the tender flesh beneath to further insult, so I continue to walk very slowly in the direction of my vehicle.

It is not until I actually get to the door of my car that I realize I am emitting a high-pitched wail. I'm not quite sure how long I have been making this vocalization, but it ends as I begin to consider the complications that will be involved in fishing my keys out of the pockets in my shorts, opening the car door and actually driving myself to the hospital.

IX.

When Colleen appeared at the hospital, I had already been treated by a doctor. My hands and chest were bandaged and I was recuperating in the burn ward. I was sedated, and so unaware of her presence for quite some time. When I did come to, the first thing I saw was Colleen's face. Through the murkiness induced by the sedative, it looked to me as if there was a third eye floating on her forehead. Thus, my first words to her were:

"Why don't you get rid of that extra eyeball?!"

Colleen looked concerned. She immediately rang for the attending nurse and then drew closer to my bed.

"How the hell did this happen?" she asked.

I chuckled. "Bad heartburn. Its just my hiatal hernia acting up!"

Colleen continued to stare at me with a serious, concerned look. She brushed her hand over my head soothingly. The doctor entered the room.

"You've suffered severe burns to your hands and your chest," the doctor said, addressing his statement both to Colleen and to me. "Can you tell me how it is that this happened?"

I repeated the joke that I previously made to Colleen when she asked me the same question.

"It's just my hiatal hernia acting up, doc."

The doctor laughed. "Well, that's the worst case of heartburn I've ever treated. But seriously, can you tell me the circumstances under which this happened? It looks like you fell into a fire."

"I was just running along a trail," I responded, "when all hell broke loose. I don't know what else to tell you. I felt sick. I puked and shit myself and then there was fire everywhere. I really don't know what happened."

The doctor looked at Colleen. It was clear that he thought I wasn't in my right mind.

"Well, let me come back once the sedation has worn off. By that time I'll have had time to look over your tests and we can talk some more."

X.

When we next saw the doctor he looked puzzled and concerned. He appeared in my hospital room with a stack of paperwork and MRI scans. He leafed through the sheets in his folder, looked up at me and then at Colleen, and then leafed through the papers once again. Finally, he scratched his head, closed the folder and spoke.

"Well, I'm not sure what to say. The results of these tests are very perplexing, and I'm not certain what to make of them or how to explain them."

I looked over at Colleen. She returned my look appearing very worried. No doubt so did I. Neither of us had ever encountered a doctor who so readily admitted his own ignorance on some medical matter.

"What is it doc? What does the scan show?"

The doctor sighed and pulled a sheet of film out of his stack of papers. He handed it to me and said, "It looks like there is some sort of abnormality in your abdomen."

The MRI scan that I now held in my hands showed the contents of my torso. I could clearly see the outline of my body, and within it a variety of organs nestled next to one another the way that you would expect them to be positioned. However, right in the area of my stomach there appeared to be some sort of object. The object had diffuse edges that shaded off into nothing. It was divided up into a series of long, pointed tendrils that seemed to be reaching upwards, toward my esophagus.

"What is that?" I said to the doctor, ignoring the fact that he had already confessed his lack of knowledge on precisely this topic.

"As I said, I don't really know."

"It looks like a flame," Colleen chimed in.

"That, of course, would be impossible," the doctor asserted.

"But she's right. It looks like there's a fire burning inside of my stomach."

The three of us looked at one another, each silent and confused. I looked at Colleen. She avoided my gaze and looked at the doctor, who in turn became uncomfortable and looked away from her and toward me. I looked away from the doctor and at Colleen, who was still looking at the doctor. Eventually we all just looked at the ground.

"The universe is eternal fire, forever rekindling itself," I said, quoting the ancient Greek philosopher, Heraclitus.

The doctor stared at me like I was crazy.

Chapter Fifteen: The Bird With the Yellow Feet

I.

The only thing that the doctors could tell me about my injury was that it was the result of fire. Further investigations into the apparent abnormality in my abdomen turned up nothing, and the origin of the fire remained mysterious.

My own research led me to discover references to something called "spontaneous human combustion, " but the more I read, the more I realized that this was just a label that covered over our ignorance of the real causes of mysterious fires like the one I was a victim to.

Doctors and scientists apply names and labels to recurrent phenomena that are not understood, and in so doing they gain a sense of control and authority, giving the impression that they know something real and true. In fact, these names and labels are often just descriptive reports. They don't get to the true source of things. They do nothing more than sum up what anyone with eyes can see. They are just words.

To say that my injuries were the result of spontaneous human combustion is simply to say that my injuries resulted from an unknown cause. I guess this is the most that anyone can say. Doctors didn't have an explanation for my mother's decline, or for Kendrick's deadly infestation, or for Richard's syndrome. Though all of their conditions had names, these names told us nothing about *why* these conditions occurred.

When it comes right down to it, everyone has to die from something. The real culprit is human finitude.

II.

During the weeks of my recovery, Colleen cared for me and helped me come to terms with my experience. The constant discomfort of the burns, and the awareness of my body's fragility, reinforced my awareness of how vulnerable and tenuous my existence really is. Having Colleen there also made me reflect on how lucky I was to actually have someone who is close to me and who is attentive to my needs. I came to an acute recognition, during this period of recuperation, that I was not alone as long as Colleen was alive and by my side.

Colleen and I had the opportunity during this time to talk once again the way that we talked when we were young.

"I remember when I first saw you in class," I said to her. "I thought you were so beautiful. When we started to hang out together, I was a bit confused. I couldn't imagine that you would be at all interested in spending time with me."

Colleen laughed. "That's funny. I had the same feelings. I got the impression that you weren't interested in me. You seemed so aloof. You acted as if I was just another one of your friends."

"Well, to tell you the truth, that was what really drew me to you. The more I was around you, the more it seemed like you were more than just a pretty face! You had the same interests, you liked the same music, you were into doing the same things as me and all of my friends. I did feel like you were my friend before anything else. I've always felt sorry for those people we know who think the people they have romantic relationships with are somehow different from those who they are friends with. That leads to a lot of trouble, I think."

"I agree," Colleen said. "It is almost as if they are unable fully to accept their girlfriends or wives or husbands or boyfriends as human beings. It seems as if they think that a love interest is a symbolic 'thing' rather than a person."

"I can't imagine ever living without you," I said to Colleen. I then began to cry.

III.

"It is hard to believe that Kendrick and Richard are gone forever. You and I, we're the only one's left from the band."

Colleen looked at the ground. "It is strange. For some reason I thought that I would die before anyone else."

"Why is that?" I asked, reaching out to her with my bandaged hand.

"I'm not sure," she responded. "I guess I just couldn't imagine a future for myself. When I looked at everyone else, it seemed that they all had some sort of goal or talent or direction in life. I never felt that way. When I thought about my own future, it was a blank; a nothing. I imagined myself just fading away and being forgotten while others moved on with their lives."

"But here we are, together," I said.

Colleen smiled. "Yes. The funny thing is that now I feel as if nothing can ever change. I'm not sure how to say it, but it feels as if we've always been together and that no matter what happens, we always will be together. Whereas in the past everything seemed so temporary, now everything seems so permanent. Even death seems like a concretization of eternity to me now. In the past I feared death as an event that takes everything away. Now it strikes me as an event that preserves our life stories by offering a finalized conclusion. Without death, it would just be one thing after another. Whereas in the past I thought of death as just a point in time, an event that looms somewhere in the future, now it feels more like the conclusion to a story. It gathers everything else together and provides sense and order to the events of life."

"That's really interesting. Intellectually I understand what you are saying; emotionally however I don't feel it. I understand that if a story went on and on without an end it would be senseless, tedious and pointless. It's only because of its termination in a conclusion that a story can be held in one's head and appreciated as a whole for what it is. Yet, when I think about the end of my life, or the end of your life, I'm filled with an incredible sense of despair and a feeling of meaninglessness. I guess the difference is that when I'm reading a story, I can only appreciate it from the outside. My life, on the other hand, is lived from the inside. When I contemplate my own life, there's no way for me to stand apart from it and regard it like I would a story or some other artwork. When the conclusion of my life arrives, I won't be here to see it. When I die, I'll be gone and so I will miss out on the final summing up."

"No, I don't think 'you' will be gone at all. Your body will be gone, yes. But 'you' are more than your body. 'You' are the experiences, the fears, the anxieties, the joys and the projects that define the course of your life. After your body dies, all of those things remain. They all happened. They can't be undone. Therefore 'you' can't be undone."

After saying this, Colleen looked at me with a smile. It was an expression that contained a mixture of sadness and hope.

IV.

As the days passed, I became more able to move and walk on my own. Between visits to the doctor, Colleen and I would pass the time, talking and walking together.

One of the places we discovered, and made our own, was a stretch of seashore not far from our house. Often we would stop there after a visit to the doctor and walk along the paved path that wound its way next to the waterfront. I would slowly waddle while Colleen patiently stayed by my side. It wasn't so much that my legs were terribly injured, but the other burns I had suffered made any sort of movement uncomfortable and difficult. Movement, however, was important according to my doctor. "You've got to keep moving if you are going to recover," he constantly reminded me. "Movement is life!" And so Colleen and I would walk as much as my condition would allow.

The waterfront reminded me of the lakeshore where my mother and I, years before, used to walk and talk. Here there was a large variety of birds constantly engaged in the task of fishing and searching for food. There were ducks floating along the surface of the waters, sandpipers thrusting their long, pointy beaks into the mud along the shore, and seagulls diving into the water periodically. All of these birds lived side by side, competing for food with one another and yet seeming to ignore one another. Their movements never interfered with the movements of the other creatures they shared the shore with, and there never seemed to be any sort of conflicts or battles between them.

V.

One bird in particular became a point of fascination for Colleen and me. It was a tall, white bird with long, thin legs that bent backwards as it walked. Its head was almost nonexistent. The only indication that the bird had a head at all was due to a slight thickening at the end of its neck. This thickened bulb sprouted something appearing to be a beak that was in close proximity to two very small, black dots, which we figured were its eyes.

Whereas the other birds congregated in abundance, this bird was singular. There were no other birds in the area that looked quite like it. As it patrolled the shore, it walked slowly in the water so that its feet disappeared beneath the lapping waves. With each step, the bird would lift its feet into the air and then plop, plop them down, one by one, into the muddy seawater. What was especially captivating to us as we observed this creature was the fact that its feet, which when beneath the muddy water were completely obscured from view, were revealed to be bright yellow in color each time that it raised them into the air. It would stroll alongside us as we walked, plop, plop, plopping its feet into and out of the waves; each movement accompanied by a yellow flash of color that would disappear just an instant after it had appeared.

VI.

There was a sense of anticipation generated in us each time that we saw this bird. When we would leave the doctor's office and head toward the shore, one or the other of us would giggle and make reference to "the bird with the yellow feet," who would soon accompany us on our stroll. As we walked, there was something captivating about watching the bird and trying to catch a glimpse of its feet during the moments that they were out the water. Those yellow feet were perplexing to us. We could see them only for an instant at a time and we wondered endlessly about why it was that such a creature had to have such brightly colored feet. Was it some sort of evolutionary adaptation or was it a random mutation serving no real purpose whatsoever? Was the bird aware of the strange color of its feet? Was it proud of them?

VII.

Plunk, plunk, plunk. The bird would thrust its feet into the waters, revealing and then concealing the brilliance of its tinted toes.

"It's such a funny animal," Colleen said. "I mean, what purpose does a thing like that have in the world? It walks along doing nothing, really, other than captivating us with its mysterious feet! And yet, it doesn't even give us a good look at them! We only get glimpses and momentary glances."

I laughed, wincing a bit from the pain as my injured chest expanded. "I know! And with that tiny head it probably doesn't even care that its life has no purpose or meaning. It walks the shoreline, day after day, just doing what it does, teasing us with its beautiful feet!"

We laughed and stopped walking. The bird turned to face us and then continued to strut down the shore.

VIII.

Weeks passed and I became well enough to return to work. Colleen and I still continued to take our walks, enjoying them because of the time that they afforded us to talk and be together.

Our friend, the bird with the yellow feet, was always there to walk with us as well. He (or she) was always alone and never seemed to be interested in fishing like the other sea birds. All it did was stroll alongside us, stopping periodically and looking around. It seemed to have no purpose, no goals, no concerns. But those feet! Those feet continued to mesmerize us.

IX.

And then, one day, the bird was gone. When Colleen and I arrived at the path, we immediately felt its absence. The seagulls and the ducks and the sand pipers were all there, but without the yellow footed bird, everything was changed.

Colleen and I still walked our usual route that day, but we were both quiet and subdued. There was no giggling or laughing.

"I wonder what happened to the bird?" Colleen said.

"I don't know," I responded, "But I already miss him."

X.

We went back to that path a few times, but we never saw that bird, or one resembling it, again.

As time moved forward, and as we fell back into our daily work routines, Colleen and I had less and less time to go for walks or to sit down and talk about our thoughts and fears and hopes.

Eventually, the yellow feet of that bird faded in our memories.

CHAPTER SIXTEEN: RESIGNATION

I.

Heraclitus claimed that the reason why corpses are cold is because their inner fire has gone out. Extinguish the soul's flame, and life comes to an end.

According to the Buddha, this is also what constitutes Nirvana. When the fire of life goes out, suffering ceases as well.

II.

I can still feel a fire burning inside of me, and though it causes distress, pain and suffering, it also pushes me forward to do things and to remain active in the world. Life is pain and suffering, as the Buddha's First Noble Truth asserts, but this is not reason enough to do away with life, because life is also activity and adventure and mystery and many other things. Life is tension and striving. It is neither good nor evil; it is both good and evil and everything in between.

III.

The pain in my stomach remains, and I have come to understand that it is intimately connected to all of the attitudes and beliefs that I hold today. It's that simple. My entire philosophy is the result of the pain in my gut. I don't need to construct an elaborate metaphysical system in order to locate the root cause of my entire mental attitude. The cause is right here in my body. It's that persistent, burning ache. That is the only truth that there is.

I really don't want this pain to stop. At this point in my life it is the only thing that motivates me to do the things that I do. Why do I bother to get up in the morning? So that I can take my medicine. Why do I go to work afterwards? Because I don't want to just sit around thinking about my discomfort. Why do I go to sleep at night? So that I can get away from the aching feeling that has been with me all day long. This malady is a double-edged sword, and that's where my ambivalence toward life stems from. Despite the inherent physical discomfort of my condition, it has at least one overwhelmingly positive consequence: it forces me to think about the meaning of life.

I have come to the conclusion that all great thoughts, acts and deeds are the result of a persistent discomfort felt in some part of the body. All human accomplishments are secondary to physical pain. Private physical discomfort is the primary motivating factor in human psychology.

IV.

My condition has never been unequivocally pinned down, diagnosed or treated. All of the doctors I have consulted claim that the incident on the trail was completely unrelated to my persistent stomach complaints; but I know that's wrong. They are related, just like all things in the world are related to one another in some way. As Heraclitus wrote, all is one. Everything pushes and pulls against everything else, and the world is just one big ball of conflict. The pain in my gut is related to the burns I suffered, which in turn are related to the death of my mother, punk rock, the death of my friends and all of my experiences growing up. All of this is related to my decision to study philosophy, to work as a teacher, my nightmares, my marriage to Colleen and to running. There are no loose ends. Everything loops back on everything else, pulling this way and that until the strings snap, all goes slack and the fire goes out.

V.

Heraclitus had another insight: nature loves to hide. Behind the things that we can see, taste, touch and feel there remains a hidden reality. This hidden world makes itself known to us in fits and stops. It allows us to peek at it for a moment before it conceals itself once again, hiding in wait until it is ready to make another appearance. We catch sight of it once in a while, but most of the time it remains veiled, and we forget about what is really true and important as we become more and more entangled in the superficialities of life. The irony is that these superficialities, like work and relationships, nightmares and music, are the very conditions that make it possible for us to engage with the deeper truth of the world. Without these, we would have no point of focus, nothing to draw and retain our attention long enough to see past the surface in order to catch a glimpse of the concealed reality that hides below. Just as you can't look at the sky in general, but must rather gaze at a particular patch or portion of the sky, so too with Being itself. You have to focus on one particular manifestation of Being in order to appreciate and contemplate how the truth of reality manifests and reveals itself. Nature loves to hide, and in knowing this we also know that we need to look for something beyond appearances.

And appearances are infinitely complicated, which means that as life goes on, there are infinitely many things to explore, investigate and delve into. What makes any of these investigations profound, however, is insight into how everything that we can experience has the potential to lead us deep into the void out of which all things emanate. My heartburn, your sprained ankle, a song, the latest pulp novel, a world war; any of these things can offer a pathway back to eternity if we allow ourselves to linger long enough in their presence so that we can catch a flicker of Being as it flashes forth and then conceals itself once again.

VI.

There are cycles and rhythms to the unfolding of life, but I don't take any sort of comfort in this. When I was a teenager, I remember observing my own internal moods as they cycled between depression and happiness. I remember thinking that when I was depressed, there was reason for optimism since the next part of the cycle led to happiness. But then when I was happy, I remember a mood of dread hovering over me as I pessimistically anticipated the onslaught of the next wave of depression. Since everything loops back on everything else, there is no firm ground on which to stand. The cycles and rhythms of life are themselves always in motion, and it would only be by stepping back and detaching ourselves from life that we could see these cycles for what they are. But it is impossible to be detached from life so long as you are living it. So long as a fire burns inside of you, there is no end to the strain and the stress, the anxiety and the tension of being alive. Only with death does the story end. It is only then that the entire trajectory of a life that has been lived can be summed up and appreciated from afar. But at that point the person who lived a particular life is gone, and so no longer able to witness the completed project.

VII.

My work at the college continues. Since getting tenure, I have struggled with the idea of how philosophy can be institutionalized and pursued as a profession. If philosophy is not about any particular thing but rather about revealing our ignorance of the real truth, is it even possible to teach philosophy? If philosophy is all about thinking new thoughts, raising new questions and boldly confronting old dogmas, how does this discipline fit in with an educational establishment? If philosophy is a form of nihilism, can it have any useful place in the mainstream? Isn't it, in essence, a reaction against the mainstream?

At times it feels like I am living a contradiction by taking a salary, living a middle class life, and reaping the respect that comes from being a professor all while encouraging students to subvert authority and to question traditional assumptions about reality. It's only by virtue of my degrees and my station of authority within the college institution that I'm granted a soapbox for the espousal of these philosophical ideas. This incongruity between my lifestyle and my teachings feels uncomfortable.

But without the backing of the institution, these ideas would have a much more limited audience. Perhaps by conveying these sorts of ideas to the people who are on track to become the future leaders of society, society itself can be changed. Instead of a sudden and violent revolution, perhaps a slow and quiet revolution can be enacted in which the mainstream population comes to be more unsure of itself, less dogmatic about what is right and what is wrong, and more open to seeing beneath superficial appearances. Maybe the message of nihilism can be spread and embraced, just as the messages of democracy, and capitalism, and communism, and consumerism have taken hold of entire populations. Maybe the place of philosophy is such that it demands to be in tension with the traditions, customs and conventions of the mainstream world.

Without tension, all things fall slack, and if philosophers did not have something to question and undermine, then it may be the case that philosophy itself would cease to burn with animating passion.

VIII.

Jesus associated with sinners precisely because they were the ones who needed to be saved.

IX.

It was the last class meeting of the semester, and as usual I devoted the session to asking the students to voice their thoughts about the course, what they had learned, and whether or not they saw themselves as philosophical thinkers.

"So how many of you would consider yourselves to be philosophers?" I asked.

About three quarters of the students in the classroom raised their hands. In my experience this was not unusual, and while it felt gratifying to see the majority of students affirm their commitment to philosophy, I also wondered how sincere they were. Were they just trying to please their teacher? Did they think that such a show of enthusiasm would improve their final grades? Or was it really true that all of these students had discovered something of value in what we had been studying?

At this point, I found myself most interested in discovering what those students who did not raise their hands were thinking. Those who made the conscious effort to refrain from raising their hands might have, it seemed to me, some form of critical perspective that could be instructive.

I called on one of the students who had not raised his hand. He was a young man, probably about nineteen or twenty years old, with brightly colored blue hair that was cut into a mohawk. His nose, lip, and left eyebrow were all pierced with silver rings. Throughout the semester, he had been very engaged in the class discussions, and I anticipated from his written work that he would get a final grade of A in the course.

"Jerod. Why don't you think of yourself as a philosopher?" I asked, smiling.

"Well, it all seems like a bunch of mental masturbation, to tell you the truth. It doesn't get you anywhere, and so it all feels frustrating. I mean, all these questions get asked, all this speculation and wonder, but where does it lead? I'm more interested a field of study like physics where you can actually work with something tangible rather than pontificating endlessly about nothing."

"So you don't see any overlap between a field like physics and philosophy?" I asked.

"Well, OK. There is overlap," the student acknowledged. "I understand that physics had its historical roots in the questions asked by the ancient Greeks. But I think today we have moved past all that. We are now closer than ever to really understanding how the physical universe works. Modern science has surpassed and left behind all of the naive thoughts of those early philosophers."

I smiled. "So what plans do you have as you study physics?"

"I eventually want to teach," the student replied.

"That's great," I responded. "So, do you want to teach at the college level?"

"Yes," Jerod answered.

"So you are going to have to pursue graduate studies?"

"Yes. I want to get a Ph.D."

"Interesting," I said. "Do you know what 'Ph.D.' stands for?"

Jerod looked at me wide-eyed. "I don't know what the letters stand for, but I know that I need that degree in order to teach where I want to teach."

"Ph.D. stands for 'Philosophy Doctor.' In order to earn that degree you need to show not only that you understand the state of your chosen field, but you must also produce a new and original piece of work. You need to question the old assumptions, raise new questions and contribute new learning to your discipline. In other words, you need to philosophize about physics if you want to earn a Ph.D. in physics," I said.

Jerod looked at me silently for a moment, his lower jaw slack. Then he shook his head slowly and laughed.

"You got me, professor!" he chuckled.

X.

Colleen remained vigilant concerning my health. She insisted that I see my doctor regularly and she made sure that I took my medication on schedule.

"I don't want you to die before me," she joked. "If that happens I'll be all alone and I'll turn into a crazy cat lady!"

"But if you die first, I'll be left behind. What would I do then?" I responded.

"Well, OK, let's die at the same time. How's that?" she said. "Just let me know when the Grim Reaper is creeping up on you and I promise to let you know if he creeps up on me first."

"That Grim Reaper; what a creep!" I snorted.

Colleen chuckled. She stretched her arms out above her head, arching them forward and curving her fingers into claws. She contorted her face into a scowl and began to let out a low-pitched moan. Then she slowly started to shamble in my direction. She had become the Grim Reaper himself.

"I'm coming to get you!" Colleen growled.

"Colleen!" I yelled with mock fright in between giggles. "He's here!"

Colleen slowly inched toward me, shuffling her feet across the floor, moaning and looming like a hungry zombie.

Our dog and cat became alarmed at all of this. The dog started to bark while the cat meowed loudly and took cover behind a chair. They seemed unable to decide whether Colleen and I were playing a game or whether there was real danger afoot. The dog jumped up on his back legs and lunged hesitantly at Colleen while the cat   mewed more and more insistently.

"It's Ok," Colleen tried to reassure the animals, but her laughter got in the way.

We laughed together, at each other, and at the reaction of our pets. The force of our outburst swelled until it was all out of proportion to the real humor of the situation. As Colleen laughed louder and more violently, I found myself swept away by the momentum, until I too was squealing uncontrollably. This growing frenzy, we both knew, was certainly indicative of some deeply repressed tension that was finally finding some relief. As the minutes went by our mirth grew even greater in intensity. It was as if our giggles, hoots and cackles were rebounding off of one another, reinforcing and energizing our laughter until we could hardly breathe.

"Oh stop!" I haltingly pleaded, panting and wheezing. "You're killing me!"

This last utterance brought our laughter to an entirely new, and unexpected, level of frenzy. I fell to the ground and Colleen collapsed onto the couch, wrapping her arms around her torso in an attempt to quiet her shrieks. Tears filled our eyes and we gasped for breath as we spasmodically and explosively snorted and howled. Eventually a crescendo was reached during which the sounds of our laughter became indistinguishable from the sounds of weeping.

Our dog circled us frantically, barking and yelping, while the cat hissed and meowed. The animals were becoming more and more agitated the louder and more out of control that our hysterics became.

"It's OK, it's OK," Colleen gasped as she tried to calm our two pets. "Everything will be OK."

Acknowledgements

Thanks to Juneko Robinson who, over the many years that I have struggled with this story, has read its successive versions, offering honest, constructive comments that have helped improve its readability, authenticity and narrative structure. Without her advice and inspiration, this book would never have been completed.

My deep, deep appreciation goes to Kent Daniels and Dario Goykovich, two good friends who have read various drafts, offering detailed criticisms and practical suggestions concerning the story's structure, organization and plausibility. They have had an enormous effect on how this book has turned out.

Thanks also to Irene Barnard for her detailed comments and suggestions on a near final version of the manuscript. Her observations about character motivation have helped to make this story more convincing, and her close reading spotted mistakes and errors that I might have otherwise overlooked.

I offer my gratitude to the following people for their willingness to read, criticize or just listen to me talk about this story over the years: Randall Lake, Jason Mcquinn, Linda and Bill Macioci, John Erdmann, Paki, Tom and Kaitlin Mowry, Stuart Jakl, Matt Schmidt, Katie Terezakis, Larry Torcello, Tom Truchan, David Rollison, Scott and Krista Lukas, Christopher Anderson, and Rob Underwood.

Finally, I lovingly acknowledge the memory of my mother, Frances Marmysz, and Juneko's mother, Nobuko Robinson; two tough immigrant women who made it possible for us to become who we are.

About the Author

John Marmysz holds a Ph.D. in philosophy from SUNY Buffalo. He currently teaches at the College of Marin in Kentfield, CA. His previous books include *The Nihilist's Notebook* (Moralinefree Publishing, 1996), *Laughing at Nothing: Humor as a Response to Nihilism* (SUNY Press, 2003), *Fear, Cultural Anxiety, and Transformation* (Lexington Books, 2009), and *The Path of Philosophy: Truth, Wonder and Distress* (Wadsworth Publishing, 2011).

In the 1980's, Marmysz was the lead singer in the San Francisco Bay Area punk rock band Sacripolitical and was publisher of the fanzine *Twilight of the Idols*. His experiences as both a punk and as a professor inform *The Nihilist*, which is his first novel.

Marmysz's blog, *The Nihilist Void*, can be found at: marmysz.wordpress. com

Made in the USA
San Bernardino, CA
18 July 2016